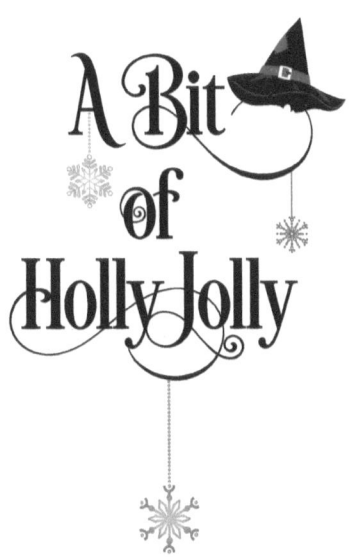

A Bit of Holly Jolly

HOLIDAZE IN SALEM

A Bit of Holly Jolly

HOLIDAZE IN SALEM

KELLY ELLIOTT

A Bit of Holly Jolly
Book 2 Holidaze in Salem © 2022 by Kelly Elliott

Cover Design by: Graphics by Stacy
Interior Design & Formatting by: Elaine York,
Allusion Publishing, www.allusionpublishing.com
Copy and Proofing Edits by: Andrea Vanryken with Yellow Bird
Editing

For more information on Kelly and her books, please visit her
website www.kellyelliottauthor.com.

Chapter One

Lucas

Two Months Ago

Shawn put a bottle of beer in front of my face and gave it a small shake. I took it and nearly downed the entire thing. I set it down next to me and stared out at the sun setting over the field behind his house.

"I called Kristin. She won't tell me anything other than Hollie doesn't want to see you right now, that she needs some time to process."

Closing my eyes, I muttered, "Fuck."

"Did you know Wendy had recorded you guys having sex?"

I turned and gaped at my best friend.

He cleared his throat. "I'll take that as a no."

"Who the fuck does that?" I asked. "Who films someone without their permission?"

"I've got a call in to my dad to see if you might be able to press charges."

I shook my head. "I've never hated anyone as much as I hate that woman. Does she think this would ever make me be with her again?"

Shawn raised his brows. "I think she's obsessed with you, and the only goal she had by sending that video was to hurt Hollie and nothing more."

"Is it wrong, I want to just...?" I clenched my fists.

"I'd feel the same way. But what Hollie needs to realize is that video was taken a long time ago. Way before the two of you got together."

I sighed. "If you were with a girl, would you want to see a video of her fucking some guy regardless of how long ago it was?"

He frowned. "Point taken. I'd want to hurt the guy."

I closed my eyes and tried to get the memory of seeing the hurt look on Hollie's face out of my mind. The fact that she wouldn't even talk to me nearly had me going insane. Not to mention the desire to go to Wendy and give her a piece of my mind.

Shawn's phone went off with a text, and he pulled it out. "It's from Kristin."

"What did she say?" I quickly asked.

Shawn looked down at his phone, then back up to me. I could see the corner of his mouth twitch slightly.

"Shawn, why do you look amused?"

Turning the phone, he showed me the text. It took me a second to move past how he had Kristin's number stored in his phone to read her message.

The Bitch: She's at the place in which I do not care to ever see you again...so don't come!

I looked at Shawn. "What in the hell is she talking about?"

"They're in the old cabin that is on Kristin's family's place. Where she used to live."

"Why can't you come?"

He looked away, then back at me, and I swore, he was blushing. "It was where I kissed her once upon a time."

My eyes widened. "You kissed Kristin? When? Why didn't you ever tell me?"

He shrugged. "It was nothing."

"If it wasn't anything, why won't she let you come then?"

Shawn rubbed at the back of his neck.

Sighing, I grabbed my keys. "Come on, you can show me where it's at and tell me on the way why Kristin doesn't want you there."

"I think I should just–"

"Right now, I don't give a shit about what happened between you and Kristin. I want to get to Hollie. Let's go."

Shawn let out a long breath and said as he followed me, "This isn't going to turn out good."

As we drove toward Kristin's parents' place outside of Salem, Shawn filled me in on what happened between the two of them four years ago.

"I was helping her father with some electrical stuff because he's best friends with my dad."

"Yes, I know that," I said as I tried not to speed.

"Anyway, they have an old cabin on their place at the back of the property, and he wanted me to take a look at the electrical box. He had some meeting he had to be in, so he gave me the keys, and I went by myself. Kristin was there, sitting on the front porch with a bottle of wine nearly finished off."

I turned to him. "Tell me, you guys didn't."

He grimaced.

"I don't even want to know right now," I said as I pulled up to the small cabin. Kristin's car was parked there but not Hollie's.

"I should probably stay in the car and, um, watch it."

Rolling my eyes, I got out of my car and raced up the two small steps that led to the porch and front door. I was about to knock when Kristin opened the door.

"She's upset with me that I told you where she was."

Looking past her, I saw Hollie sitting on a small love-seat, her legs pulled up and tucked close to her body. She was staring out a large picture window that overlooked a hill with a creek that flowed through it. The cabin was actually really cute; I could see why Kristin had lived here.

"Thanks, Kristin."

She nodded and squeezed my hand. Then she looked past me and frowned. "That jerk came anyway!"

When she stormed down out of the door and toward my car, I shut the door to the cabin and walked over to Hollie.

I bent down in front of her. "Hey."

She turned and looked at me, and my breath caught in my throat. Her eyes were swollen and red from crying.

My heart felt like it had twisted in my chest. "Hollie, baby."

I placed my hand on the side of her face, and she leaned into my touch. "I know, I shouldn't have run. I was so stunned and hurt. I didn't know what else to do. Seeing you with her like that, it..."

I placed my finger to her lips to silence her. "I know and I'm so sorry. I had no idea she had, she had...filmed us at any time—you need to know that. I would never do anything like that."

Hollie nodded. "I know you wouldn't."

Pulling her down onto my lap I sat on the floor. "I need you to know, Hollie, that it meant nothing. It was just sex with Wendy. That's all. I've never had feelings for her, and that video was clearly taken a long time ago."

Hollie nodded and sniffled. "I know that too. I have to be honest with you, Lucas. I want to cast a spell on that bitch."

I fought to hold back a smile. "Well, considering you simply hoped she would get a rash, and she did, I would hate to think of what you could do when you're this upset."

An evil smile grew on her beautiful face. "Just one little hex. I really do need the practice."

"Hollie," I warned.

With a roll of her eyes, she sighed and leaned her forehead against mine. "I think the best revenge is to not let her know it got to me even though I totally acted like a child and ran from you. An adult would have stayed and talked about it."

"I agree on the revenge part." I kissed her forehead and added, "I hate to say this, but I don't think this will be the last we hear of Wendy."

Hollie drew back and locked her gaze with mine. "Because she's obsessed with you?"

I flinched. "Something like that."

"Fine, I'm going to let this one go, but so help me, Lucas, if she does another stunt like this, I'm going full-on bat-witch crazy on her ass."

Laughing, I slid my hand around her neck and brought her lips to mine, kissing her softly at first. Soon, our kiss turned deeper. Hollie pulled back and drew in a breath of air. "We better stop or Kristin might walk in on something she doesn't want to see. I think I might have scared her by showing her the video. She did say you have a really nice ass, though, which I agreed with."

My eyes closed and I slowly shook my head. "Can we please delete it?"

"Oh, I did—the second Kristin said that."

The door to the cabin flew open, causing Hollie and me to both turn and see Kristin marching in, Shawn hot on her trail.

"You are the biggest asshole I've ever met!"

9

"And you're the biggest bitch!"

Kristin gasped. "Did you just call me fat?"

Shawn stepped back as if Kristin just slapped him. "What? How in the hell did you get that out of me calling you a bitch?"

With her hands now firmly on her hips, Kristin replied, "You said, 'biggest.'"

Shawn groaned as he rolled his eyes.

"Oh, dear," Hollie softly said as I helped her up.

"I'm sorry, you got *that* out of me calling you a bitch?" Shawn asked, confused.

"So, you admit, you think I'm fat."

"What's happening?" I whispered as I leaned in toward Hollie. I did a double-take when I saw her smiling at Kristin and Shawn. "I don't like that look on your face, Hollie."

Turning, she winked. "What look?"

Then, spinning back to face the two other people in the room who had clearly lost their minds, she walked toward them, all thoughts of Wendy and the video seeming to have vanished from her thoughts.

"Well, well, well. What is going on here?"

When Kristin and Shawn both turned and looked at Hollie, Kristin narrowed her eyes and pointed.

"Oh, no. No, no, no, Hollie Craft. Don't even think it!"

Shawn threw his hands up in the air, clearly just as confused as me. "What in the living hell is going on here?"

Hollie wore a shit-eating grin on her face.

"Hollie, don't even think about it."

"Wait," Shawn said as he waved his hands around. "Are we all still upset about Wendy and the video that shall never be discussed, or is this because I called Kristin fat?"

I closed my eyes. *Oh, Shawn, you stupid bastard.*

Kristin gasped.

"No, wait, wait, wait! I didn't call her fat, but she thinks I called her fat, so are you giving me that weird look because of that? Because I didn't call you fat!" Shawn yelled as he pointed to Kristin. "You have one of the hottest bodies I've ever seen!"

That seemed to cool Kristin off almost instantly. "You think I'm hot?"

Shawn looked exasperated, poor guy. "Yes!"

Kristin blushed, then cleared her throat. "I still can't stand you."

When I looked at Hollie, she was tapping her finger to her chin and somehow...just somehow, I knew my little witch was plotting.

Chapter Two

Hollie

"Hollie, you have to come over for dinner tonight, sweetheart, and I won't take no for an answer. I have my ways of making you come, you know."

My mother, Elaine Craft, who, only just two short months ago, I discovered had been a practicing witch in the closet, was clearly not going to give up on me attending family dinner night.

"Are you seriously threatening me with what I think you are?"

"Don't be silly, sweetheart. Now, dinner will be at six sharp. I'll expect you and Lucas."

I groaned. "Mom, I have three Christmas parties I'm doing between now and Christmas. I have so much work to do."

"I see. If work is that important, more important than your family..."

Feeling her anger through the phone, I drew in a deep breath. "We'll be there."

"That's my girl! Do me a favor, stop by the store, and pick up some of that rosemary bread your father adores. He claims I don't make it the same way, and it will go good with dinner tonight."

"Sure thing, Mom."

"Talk soon and love you!"

"Love you too."

I hit End and dropped back onto the bed. Grabbing a pillow, I buried it over my face and screamed into it.

"Feel better?" Lucas asked as I felt the bed dip and his body move over mine. An instant rush of heat swept over me, and my lower stomach pulled with desire.

Tossing the pillow to the side, I looked into his caramel eyes and nearly melted. "No, but I have a feeling you know of a way to make me feel better."

When his gaze flicked over to the tableside clock, he focused back on me and grinned. "I've got a few extra minutes this morning."

"Oh, yeah? What did you have in mind?"

"Eating my breakfast slowly at first and then finishing off with a bang."

My entire body heated as he pushed open my robe and kissed me softly. When his lips moved down my neck to my breast, I gasped and laced my fingers in his hair.

"Lucas," I hissed as I spread my legs and lifted my hips in a silent plea.

He cupped my other breast and pinched the nipple as he sucked on the opposite one. I closed my eyes and arched my back, pushing further into his mouth.

When his mouth moved down my stomach, my breathing increased. I lifted my head and watched him place a soft kiss on each side of my inner thigh. Flicking his eyes up to me, he smiled, and I bit down on my lip.

"Lucas, don't stop," I panted as my fingers pushed into his soft hair and pulled him closer to me. I wasn't even embarrassed that I was grinding against his face. "God, it feels so good, but I need more!"

Always the one to want to please, Lucas flicked my clit faster with his tongue as he pushed his fingers inside me. I jumped and felt my hips moving faster.

"Yes! I'm so close."

Then he placed his tongue over my clit as he curled his fingers inside me. I exploded and cried out his name as I fell into a euphoria that seemed to steal the air from the room.

It took me a few moments to fall back to reality as Lucas unzipped his pants and pushed inside of me.

"Oh, God!" I called out as another orgasm wracked through my body.

"Jesus, Hollie," Lucas said as he lost himself in me. I loved when he made love to me. It was sweet and passionate, and I could feel the love he had for me. But moments like this, when he lost control and took me hard and fast, those were the moments my body reacted in the most delicious of ways.

"I feel you coming around me," he said as he locked his mouth over mine. Only a few seconds later, he broke the kiss and cried out my name as he came.

Once he stopped, he held his weight off me and drew in deep breaths of air.

Locking his gaze with mine, he growled, "Fuck, you're so addictive. I can't get enough of you."

My fingers laced through his hair as a contentment moved over me. I could honestly crawl back into bed and drift off to sleep, I was that relaxed.

"I feel the same. I wish we could get under the covers and stay in bed all day."

He drew back and smiled before he kissed me softly on the lips. "Soon. Two more weeks and you and I are off for vacation."

I sighed and dropped my arms onto the bed. "That's too long! I want it to be the day after Christmas now!"

Kissing me on the nose, Lucas pushed off me and reached for my hand, pulling me up. "I need to get cleaned up. I have a meeting this morning."

My mouth fell open. "You're going to be late!"

"Knowing I'll have the taste of you still on my tongue during the meeting will make it worth it."

Laughing, I shook my head as I watched him clean himself off and then hand me a warm washcloth to do the same.

"No coffee then?"

"Nope, already drank a cup. Listen, I need to go. Dinner at your folks tonight?"

Groaning, I nodded. "Yes. Do you need to meet there, or can we drive together?"

"I'll be home earlier. You?" he asked.

"I've got three meetings today with clients, but I'll be finished up around one."

He pulled me to him and kissed me. Lord, the man could kiss me senseless.

"I love you. See you later."

As I attempted to remember how to think clearly after that kiss, I replied, "I love you too. See ya."

Seeing as I was going to be late myself, I quickly got dressed, fixed my hair, and made a cup of coffee to go.

"I need this Christmas party to be the talk of the town," Susan Althorp stated as we walked around the large event center she had rented.

I smiled and pulled out my notebook, where I kept all my notes for each client. "As per our previous conversations, the event is to raise money for the Boston Children's Hospital, and you wanted it to be a fun, light-hearted event. I went ahead and drew up some sketches of the table design you approved, but I'd like for you to get a feel for what they'll look like so if you want anything changed, we can do that ASAP."

Susan grinned, took the drawing from me, and then gasped. "Oh, Hollie, you really are so very talented. I've never had an event planner give me anything like this before."

I couldn't help but feel a sense of pride as she stared down at the colored drawing.

"Thank you for your kind words. As you can see, I've kept it fun, with a few touches of glamor in there as well. The LED balloons are a simple touch, yet they give the room a more luminous feel. At the entrance of the room, tall Christmas tree balloons will greet your guests before they walk into a beautiful sea of reds, whites, and greens. Each table will have these handmade snowmen on them. Each hat will have the table number on it and will also serve as a candy cane holder. The plates will be made to look like snowmen, using a smaller salad plate as the head and the dinner plate as the body. Raisins for the eyes and buttons, and a small, felt carrot for the nose. The napkins will be folded like the top of the hat, with the knife being the rim. The fork and spoon are the arms."

Sharon slowly shook her head. "That is the cutest thing I've ever seen."

"You mentioned you love the grab-and-go charcuterie jars that I used at another party."

"Yes! I love that idea."

"So, I think we can do small little jars and fill them with a bit of fruit, nuts, a long pretzel with deli meat, and top it with a cheese wedge."

"Love it!"

"The dessert bar will feature the large snowman cake sitting on a red sleigh. I was thinking some lighted trees, white and red, scattered throughout the desserts. All the plates will be white to showcase the colors of the desserts. I'd really like to use the cake as well as the desserts as a decoration focus."

She nodded. "I love it!"

"The tables will all have white tablecloths and black napkins—which, again, are the hats for the snowmen. The dessert table will have red napkins as you requested."

"Hollie, you are amazing. This is going to be the best charity dinner I've ever thrown!"

"Any changes?"

"No!" she gasped. "Do not change a thing!"

Laughing, I put my notebook back in my bag. "In that case, I will head on out to my next appointment. If you change your mind on anything or want to add something, please let me know as soon as possible. I'll be there the morning of set-up, and you'll have my cell phone if you need anything."

Susan gave me a hug and stepped back. "Thank you again, Hollie. I couldn't have done this without you."

"It was my pleasure, Susan. Talk soon!"

I quickly called and checked my voice messages, then slipped into my car and headed to my next appointment. A front was moving in, and they were talking about a pretty good chance of snow, so I wanted to get everything taken care of before it started coming down.

"It would be a pity if I had to miss dinner at my folks tonight because of a storm!" I said to myself.

My next appointment was with the City of Salem. They were having a Christmas party for all city employees that was Grinch-themed, and I was the lead party planner handling the decorations and the dinner. A job I took very seriously, especially since one of the city councilmen from Boston would be in attendance. If I could land something with the City of Boston, that would be amazing!

As I walked into the meeting room, I came to an abrupt halt. Lucas was leaning against the wall talking with another guy who appeared to be about the same age as us. Before I could say anything, a voice from my left said, "Ms. Craft, it's such a pleasure to see you again."

Lucas turned and saw me right as I looked at Tammy Larson, the woman in charge of the planning for the city Christmas party.

"Hello, Tammy, it's nice to see you again."

"My last meeting ran over, and I was chatting with some friends."

Sweeping my gaze past Tammy, I couldn't help but smile when Lucas winked at me. He made his way over to me, never once looking anywhere other than my eyes. Leaning down, he brushed his lips over mine tenderly.

"Long time, no see. How was your first meeting?"

Feeling my cheeks heat, I quickly looked at Tammy, then back to Lucas. "It went great."

"Are you free for lunch?"

"Considering my next appointment is with your mother, I think so."

Lucas laughed. "Call me when you're done here. I'll wait for you in the lobby."

I gave him a nod and focused back on Tammy. She seemed amused.

"I take it you know Lucas?" she asked with a chuckle.

"Yes, he's my boyfriend."

Tammy motioned for me to follow her. "Let's talk and walk."

Following her, I saw her glance over her shoulder. "You're the reason he's been so happy lately."

Okay, if I was embarrassed seconds ago, I was mortified now. Deciding it would be best to change the subject, I launched into the party details.

"I got your email that mentioned you approved the Whoville idea. I have a lot of the decorations at my warehouse, including the crooked trees that I thought would look really cute at the entrance."

"Will you be attending the party?" Tammy asked as she grabbed her laptop, and we headed out of the meeting room and down the hall to her office.

"Me?" I asked.

"I'm assuming, since you're dating Lucas, you'll be coming to the party with him."

"Oh," I said with a nervous laugh. "His mother is throwing a bridal shower for her son and his fiancé the same night as the Whoville party. I believe we're going to that."

Tammy walked into her office and sat down behind her large walnut desk, motioning for me to sit in one of the two chairs on the other side of it. "Take a seat."

Sitting, I pulled out my notebook and pencil before I looked back at her. "Did you have any last-minute requests that you'd like to make or any questions?"

Tammy leaned back in her chair and smiled. "No. I looked over the photos you sent me a few months ago once again, and I loved everything you did for the previous Grinch party. I like your idea of doing the table decorations with stacked presents, and your notion of using all recyclable dinnerware went over great as I told you before."

"Great! And you found some volunteers that are willing to do the plasticware like the picture I sent?"

"Yep, it's called my teenage daughter and her friends. They're excited about the party, though, and are happy to help out."

Smiling, I said, "That's great! The company I hired for the balloons will take care of all the arches and the other balloon displays so you won't have to worry about that. I'll have the large recycle bins placed around the room so it will be easy for people to put their items in there. Were you still planning on doing the secret Santa?"

"Yes. And I think the idea of using the Christmas tree already up in that room is a great idea. I'm not sure if you walked over and saw that they decorated it like the picture you sent."

"I hadn't had a chance to go see, but that's great. So, no changes? We're a go for all the plans?"

Tammy smiled. "No changes. And thank you for recommending the catering company. They've been amazing so far, and I think their food will be heavenly based on the samples I've tried."

"Wonderful!" I said with a wide smile as I put my notebook up. "If you don't have any concerns, then I think we are finished. Mindy, one of my assistants, will be here the morning of the party to make sure everything is set up the right way. You've requested she stay the entire party, and she has confirmed she will be able to. She knows how to get in touch with me should a problem arise."

We both stood. Reaching her hand across her desk, Tammy said, "Thank you, Hollie. You really are the party-planning queen."

Letting out a small laugh, I replied, "I try!"

"Enjoy your lunch with Lucas."

"Thank you!"

I quickly made my way to the lobby and smiled when I saw Lucas sitting in a chair scrolling on his phone. When he looked up, my breath caught. I wasn't sure if I would ever get used to that look on his face when he saw me. My heart hammered a bit more in my chest as I approached him.

"Thanks for waiting," I said.

He stood and kissed me softly on the lips. "Everything good with the Christmas party?"

Nodding, I slipped my arm through his as we made our way out of the building.

"Everything is great. She loves everything and didn't have any changes. The next appointment is the one I'm kind of stressing about."

Lucas laughed. "With Mom and Janet? Don't be stressed. Hollie, you're one of the most talented people I've ever met, and you're freaking amazing at your job."

I bumped into him lightly. "You have to say that—you're my boyfriend. Anyway, your mom will be glad to see you. Did you tell her you were coming along?"

"Nah," he said with a shake of his head. "Thought I would surprise her. Are you guys meeting somewhere?"

"Yes. We're meeting at the Village Tavern."

Smiling, Lucas opened my car door. "Oh, man, I freaking love their wings."

Before I slipped into the driver's seat, I reached up and kissed him. "See you in a few minutes. Be careful driving."

"You too, babe."

I made it to the restaurant before Lucas and was seated at the table with Rose and her future daughter-in-law Janet when Lucas walked up. Rose's eyes lit up when she saw her son walking toward us.

"Lucas," she said as she stood and kissed him on the cheek. "I was so happy when Hollie said you would be joining us."

"Any chance to spend some time with my two girls," Lucas said as he glanced over to Janet. "Sorry, Janet, I don't think Greg would like me referring you to my girl."

Laughing, Janet waved Lucas off.

"I ordered you a water," I said with a soft smile.

The waitress brought the drinks to the table and then asked if we were ready to order. Rose and I both got the lobster roll while Lucas got wings with fries, and Janet ordered a salad.

"I'll never fit into my wedding dress if I keep eating like I have been."

"You look beautiful, Janet," I stated as I did a double-take toward the front door. Kristin and Shawn walked in...together. Shawn placed his hand on Kristin's lower back as they followed the hostess.

"Do you see that?" I asked with a bit too much excitement in my voice. "They're not fighting."

"That we know of," Lucas deadpanned.

"Look! He had his hand on her back!"

Rose and Janet both looked confused. "And that's a good thing, I take it?" Janet asked.

"They are so into each other, but neither will admit it," I said, then gasped. "Oh, my God! What if they are secretly seeing one another?"

Lucas laughed. "Why would they do it in secret?"

"Yes, why?" Rose asked.

With a shrug, I replied, "I don't know. It just seemed like more of a fun idea."

"Wait," Janet said, "I'm confused. Do they like each other or not?"

I tore my gaze away from our two best friends. "They act like they can't stand each other. I mean, they bicker back and forth. I don't think I've ever seen them be civil to each other."

Taking a sip of her Coke, Rose mumbled, "Boy, does that sound familiar."

I shot her a cheeky grin while Lucas smiled.

"Oh, it looks like they aren't getting along," Janet stated as Lucas and I both snapped our heads to look back over there.

I huffed. "Ugh. If they aren't going to get along, why would they have lunch together?"

"Do they work together?" Rose asked.

Lucas cleared his throat. "No. Kristin is a first-grade teacher, and Shawn is a financial advisor."

"So why do you think they're together?" Janet asked.

I noticed out of the corner of my eye Lucas giving his mother a pleading look.

"Hollie, I showed Janet the drawings you left for your idea for the Christmas-themed bridal shower."

"Yes!" Janet said, excited. "I love them so much, Holly! The square plates with the bow around them to make them look like presents is the cutest thing ever. I love the idea of doing another holiday-themed event since our engagement was based around Halloween! I was wondering if we could add some Christmas music to play in the background?"

I nodded, but my eyes kept drifting over to Shawn and Kristin, who were very much arguing. Lucas pulled out his phone, and it was then that Rose attempted to pull me into another conversation about the bridal shower.

"I can make that change, no problem," I said as I jotted down some notes in the handy-dandy notebook she carried everywhere with her.

Glancing over to Kristin and Shawn, I saw them with their heads bent together. *What in the world is going on with those two?*

When the waitress brought our food over, I peeked over to where Kristin and Shawn were once again. Narrowing my eyes as I studied them, I asked Lucas, "What do you think they're doing? They look like they're deep in conversation."

He shrugged. "With those two, who knows?"

Something inside of me said they were both up to something. "I have to know!"

"Wait, Hollie," Lucas said as he reached for my arm to keep me seated. "Our food just got here."

"Where are you going, dear?" Rose asked.

Giving both Rose and Janet an apologetic smile, I said, "I'll be right back. I just have to find out what's going on with Kristin and Shawn!"

Before Lucas could even stop me, I was marching across the restaurant.

Chapter Three

Hollie

I stood in front of the table where Kristin and Shawn sat, both looking up at me with surprised expressions.

"Hey, guys, what brings the two of you here?" I asked as I eyed them both suspiciously.

"Oh, hey, there, Hollie," Kristin replied, a wide smile spread across her face. "What brings you here?"

With my brows furrowed, I said, "I asked you first."

Kristin let out a soft laugh. "Shawn here agreed to help me with my taxes. I had a problem with my CPA last year and have no idea how to make heads or tails out of it. Unfortunately for me, he's the only guy I know who is good with numbers."

I looked at Shawn. "You're helping her with her taxes?"

"Trying to. She's so freaking hardheaded, she seems to think she knows more about it than I do."

Kristin shot him a dirty look. "I'm a woman, so I would know more about it than you would."

He huffed.

I folded my arms over my chest. "You know stocks and stuff like that. Do you really think you're qualified to help her with her taxes?"

Shawn placed his hand over his head and acted as if he was wounded. "I'm really hurt, Hollie. In case you forgot, I have a bachelor's degree in accounting and finance."

"Overachiever," Kristin mumbled.

"I heard that, brat."

Kristin's mouth dropped open. "Did you really call me a brat?"

"Another B-word popped into my head, but I decided to be nice today."

I was positive Kristin had steam coming out of her ears. "You arrogant—"

"Oookay, I think this was a bad decision on both of your parts. The two of you are like oil and water, you don't go together."

Kristin looked at Shawn and stuck her tongue out.

"Really, Kristin?" I said with a look of disapproval.

Forcing herself to smile, Kristin looked past me. "Go enjoy your lunch, Hollie. Asshat and I will be fine."

Shawn rolled his eyes as he reached for his drink.

Sighing, I looked at both of them. "I don't know why you two don't get along."

When they exchanged a look, I saw something. Something they both tried to hide, but it slipped through for the briefest of moments. I couldn't help but smile.

"Go enjoy your lunch, Hollie. I promise we won't kill one another."

I looked between the two of them, and when I didn't say anything and instead only stood there grinning like an idiot, Kristin slowly shook her head. "Whatever it is you think you know, you are so not right on this, Hollie. So you might as well put that thought out of your head and go back to your lunch."

Shawn stared at her. "What in the hell did you just say?"

Dismissing him with a flick of her hand, Kristin gave me a warning look. "I mean it, Hollie."

I lifted my hands up. "Fine. Fine. If you say so, but I say I saw what I saw, and it was an eye-opener and something I think we need to talk about later."

"No, we don't."

Shawn pinched the bridge of his nose and slowly exhaled. "I'm going to need a double shot of whiskey and Tylenol when this day is over."

I walked out of the bathroom and crawled onto the bed. Lucas was looking over some pictures that one of his former college professors sent him of some dig site.

"I still say there is something there between them, Lucas."

He drew his brows in tight as he studied one of the photos. It was of some giant round rock or something they found in Ireland.

"You didn't see the way they looked at each other, like they wanted one another but neither one of them would even dare to admit it."

"Really?" Lucas said as he turned the photo 90 degrees and steadied it.

"Yes! And I know something happened between them in the past. What if they secretly like each other like we did! They're both fighting it so hard, maybe they need a little... push. You know, like we had."

"Uh-huh."

"So, you think I should look into it more?"

"If you think so," he replied holding up another photo of something that looked like a bowl.

"Well, I have been practicing some simple spells with Sarah. She's a sucker for love. I'm sure she'll help me with a spell to...*gently* push Kristin and Shawn together."

"Sounds good, babe."

I squealed and threw my arms around him. "I'm so glad you agree and you're on board with me using magick for this!"

Turning, I jumped off the bed and rushed out of the bedroom to grab my cell phone. I had some planning I needed to do.

"Wait, what did you say?" Lucas called after me. "You're using magick for what?"

"Just study your picture, sweetheart! I've got this!"

Picking up my cell, I hit my sister's phone number.

"Hey, what's up?"

"Okay, so I spoke with Lucas, and he is in total agreement on this. I want to put a spell on Kristin and Lucas."

My sister let out an overly dramatic sigh. "Okay, do we have to go over the rules again, Hollie? You can't just run around putting spells on people!"

"I know that! I only want a simple little spell to kind of push them together. They're both crushing on each other, Sarah. It's like I'm looking in a mirror at me and Lucas from a few months ago."

There was a silence before she asked, "Did you ask Kristin and Lucas if you could put a spell on them?"

When I didn't answer, she laughed. "Why am I not surprised?"

"Come on, Sarah! Hold on, let me find my good witch's guidebook."

"I told Lucy not to give that to you!"

I giggled as I flipped through the book.

"Found them! Okay, we can use the notice me spell, which is what I thought I was using on Lucas, but that still turned out in my favor. Have I mentioned how hot the sex is? You really should use this spell, Sarah."

"I'm going to ignore everything you just said," my sister stated dryly.

"Then we have the 'Small-Shell Love Charm.' Ohhhh... this one sounds good!"

"No, you need Kristin or Lucas to do that spell, Hollie."

Pouting, I replied, "Right. Right. Okay, then I'll do the notice me spell. I just need a picture of Lucas."

"Oh, God, what have I done? Hollie, I don't think you should do either spell. You cannot mess with free will...remember?"

"I know! I'm not. I'm simply trying to get the two of them to get their heads out of their asses."

Sarah let out a low growl. "Listen to me, Hollie. To do the notice me spell, you need to have Kristin do it, not you."

"Can't I just use their names and pictures?"

When she didn't answer, I fist-pumped. "I can! Perfect! How do I do that?"

"Hollie," Sarah warned in that annoying mother voice of hers. "You cannot do it. The last thing you need to be doing is messing around with spells. Lucy already told you that your gift is very powerful. Look at what happened to Lucas."

I flinched. My spell to get Lucas to notice me had gone all wrong, and I had ended up putting a hex on him instead. I still felt terrible about it.

"That won't happen again. I've already learned so much from you and Lucy. Besides, you'll help me to make sure I do it right. Right?"

"Wrong. I will not help you."

Instead of letting my anger get the better of me, another idea popped into my head. I needed to throw my sister off my scent.

Letting out a sigh, I put forth my best acting skills. "You're right. I got carried away."

"Wait, you're giving up on this way too easily. What are you up to, Hollie Craft?"

Laughing, I replied, "Jeesh, thanks so much for having confidence in me."

"I know you, Hollie. And I know you're not going to let this go."

Before she could lecture me anymore, I called out, "Coming! Hey, Lucas needs me. We'll chat later!"

"Hollie, wait!"

"Toodles!"

Hitting End, I smiled and hit my mother's number and waited for her to answer.

"Sweetheart, I've been expecting your call."

Grinning like a fool, I blurted out, "I need your help with a spell."

I could almost hear her nodding. "Tomorrow, nine in the morning."

"I'll be there!"

Chapter Four

Hollie

"How did you learn what all of this stuff does?" I asked as I leaned down and smelled some lavender in my mother's greenhouse.

"I learned it from my mother who learned it from her mother. And so on."

Sliding onto a stool, I watched as my mother moved about in her happy space. I realized she was totally in her element. How had I never noticed it before?

"Was it hard, hiding who you really were from me?"

Pausing, she turned to face me. "At times. I always believed that when you were ready, you'd find your gift."

I smiled, then frowned. "What if...? What if I don't know how to use it? I mean, I answer people before they even ask a question or make a comment. Some don't pay any attention to it. Other people look at me like I'm some kind of weirdo. And the last couple of weeks, I've seen things in my head before they even happen."

She leaned against a table as she watched me intently. "That's happened to you before when you were younger. Does that scare you?"

Thinking about her question, I shook my head. "No. It feels..."

My voice trailed off.

"Normal?"

I nodded. "Yes!"

"Have you talked to Sarah or Lucy about your visions? Or Lucas?"

"Lucas? I can't tell Lucas about that."

She looked confused. "Why not?"

"Mom, if I tell him I see things before they happen, he'll think I'm losing my mind!"

Laughing, she pushed off the counter. "He loves you and won't think that. Your father never thought I was losing my mind."

My mouth fell open. "You have visions?"

"No, I don't have that gift. I can sense things. Like last night, I knew you'd be calling me, and you did. But the first time I told your father I was a witch, I think he laughed for about ten minutes before he realized I was being serious."

Smiling once again, I thought of the night I brought Lucas home from the hospital and told him we needed to do a reversal spell. No doubt about it, he thought I was crazy.

"I don't know. It's only happened twice since I came to the dark side."

"Hollie Craft, do not say that. There is nothing dark about it."

I sighed. "I know, I'm just kidding. Speaking of spells..."

"Oh, were we talking about spells?"

Giving her a smirk, I pulled out the spell I had copied down. "Can I do this spell—but for two other people besides myself?"

Mom read it and shook her head. "No, if you try to, something could do wrong."

Chewing on my thumbnail, I wanted to let out a frustrated groan but instead said, "That's what Sarah said."

Mom raised a single brow. "Did you think I would have something different to say?"

I shrugged. "I was kind of hoping you would."

She shook her head, pulled out a plant from under the table, and began working on transplanting it into a bigger pot. "Who are you trying to play matchmaker with?"

"Kristin and Shawn. I know something happened between them in the past. But they fight like cats and dogs and look at each other like they want to rip their clothes off, not their heads. It reminds me of Lucas and myself."

"And that makes you think they like one another."

"No, what makes me think that is the way they look at each other. When neither of them thinks anyone is watching, they stare at one another. And not just a normal kind of stare that says I hate you and wish you would fall in a hole."

Her eyes went wide. "That's a normal kind of stare?"

"Well, if you despise the other person, it is. But they don't, because they look at each other like 'I want to get you naked in a bed and do naughty things to you.'"

Mom looked up and opened her mouth to say something, then shut it for a few moments before she spoke again.

"Here's a crazy thought—why don't you talk to Kristin and see if she wants to do the charm?"

I laughed. "Mom, this is Kristin we're talking about. Her pride alone would keep her from doing it. And if I can't do it for her, I need to figure out a way to get her to do it without her really knowing we're doing it."

Mom blinked a few times and shook her head before she picked up some cutters and started pruning a plant.

I let out a long, exhausted sigh.

"Well, you could always get her drunk and do the spell. Worked for you and Lucas."

Sitting up straight, I felt my face break out into a wide grin. "That's it! Mom, you're so smart!"

She looked over at me. "Honey, I was kidding."

Jumping off the stool, I rushed over and hugged her. "This is perfect! Kristin will use any excuse to drink wine and get drunk! *Eeeep!* This is totally going to work! I need to run and get everything for the spell. Oh! Do you have fresh cloves and nutmeg?"

"Um...wait, Hollie, I think we need to slow down for a minute."

"It's okay, I'll pick some up at Lucy's. I'm sure she has the good shit!"

My mother shook her head frantically. "The good shit? It's just normal clove and nutmeg, Hollie."

"Got to run," I said as I kissed my mother on the cheek. "Thanks for all your help, Mom. I knew I could count on you!"

As I made my way out of Mom's greenhouse, I thought I heard her say, "Oh, dear, this isn't going to turn out well." I ignored her and rushed through the house, calling out good-bye to my dad.

I hit Lucas's name in my contacts list and waited for him to answer.

"Hey, how was your visit with your mom?"

"Great! Listen, do you mind if I see if Kristin wants to have a girls' night tonight?"

"I don't mind at all. Shawn actually texted me earlier to see if I wanted to get together with a few of the guys for poker night."

"That's perfect!" I nearly shouted.

Lucas laughed. "You must really need a girls' night."

"It's going to be magical!"

Pausing, Lucas must have gotten up and shut his office door. I heard a click, then he asked, "Hollie, what are you up to?"

"What do you mean?"

"You're up to something. I can hear it in your voice."

"We talked about it last night, and you were on board with it."

"Wait," he said. I could almost picture him pinching the bridge of his nose. "What did we talk about, and when last night did we talk about it?"

"You know, Kristin and Shawn and how they secretly like one another. It was when I came out of the bathroom, and you were looking at the photos from that dig in Ireland."

Lucas paused for a moment. "I don't remember talking about Kristin and Shawn. Oh, wait. You said something about using magick. Hollie...what are you going to do?"

"Listen, you have a good time tonight, and don't worry about anything. I went over this with my mom, and you know how responsible she is."

"I have an idea—why don't we just let the two of them figure things out on their own?"

Laughing, I replied, "It's almost Christmas, and then there is New Year's."

"What does New Year's have to do with this?"

"Hello! New Year's Eve kiss?"

Lucas exhaled. "Promise me, if you do a spell, you'll do it the right way."

"Of course, I will! I've got to run. Lots to do."

"Hollie, promise me, there won't be any hexes."

"Cross my heart. I love you!"

"I love you too."

When I hit End, I drew in a deep breath and exhaled. "At least, I hope there won't be any hexes."

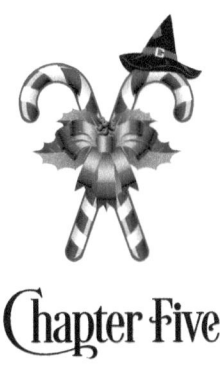

Chapter Five

Lucas

Shawn opened the door with a wide smile, and I actually felt sorry for the poor bastard. I had no idea what Hollie was up to, but if it involved another girls' night, alcohol, and spells, Shawn would either be in love by tomorrow or falling down a flight of stairs. At this point, I wasn't sure which he would prefer.

"Hey, why the worried look on your face?" he asked.

I quickly shook off where my thoughts had been. "Long day at work is all."

He slapped me on the back as I walked in. "Well, I hope you're ready to lose some money."

I let out a humorless laugh. "Someone is going to lose something, that's for sure."

His brows drew in, a confused look coming over his face. "What?"

Waving off my comment, I replied, "Nothing. Ignore me."

As I followed my best friend through his house and to the formal dining room, I debated whether I should tell him what Hollie was up to.

When I stepped into the room, I saw three other people sitting around the card table. James, Henry, and Alex, all friends from high school, glanced up as we walked into the room.

James pointed to me as he said, "I hope you came prepared to lose some money, Lucas. I'm feeling lucky tonight."

Anyone who played poker with me knew I sucked at it. I was prepared to drop some bills tonight, so their teasing never bothered me.

Henry and Lucas both laughed. "I think Lucas has come to accept he sucks at poker," Alex said.

"Is that why you guys invite me? To get my money?" I asked as I tossed my coat over the chair in the corner. I checked my phone before I turned it to vibrate. Nothing from Hollie. I wasn't sure if that was a good thing or not. Kristin was most likely already at the house. I looked at Shawn as he laughed at something James had said to him. Poor bastard. I really should warn him.

"I'm telling you, I think you'd like her, Shawn," James said as he slid the deck of cards over to me to split.

"Like who?" I asked as Shawn handed me my chips.

"Someone James works with, and I already told you, I'm not interested," Shawn answered.

I narrowed my eyes at Shawn. When he saw me staring at him, he asked, "Why are you looking at me like that?"

"Why aren't you interested in her?"

He blinked a few times, then shrugged. "I don't know."

"I'm telling you, dude, she's not looking for anything but sex. I heard she likes it dirty."

Alex sighed. "I hate being the only married guy in the bunch."

"Are you saying you're not happy with your wife?" Shawn asked.

"Hell, no, I'm not saying that. I've never been happier. I just know those days are over. Doesn't mean I want it. It's just gone. That sucks."

I laughed. "Well, you get to go home to a beautiful wife each day. Someone to share your day with."

"So do you, from what I hear. Sounds like you and Hollie are pretty serious," James said as he waggled his brows.

"Yeah, we're serious. I'm actually going to be asking her to marry me."

"Holy shit, dude," Alex said as he gave me a clap on the back. "That's awesome. When?"

I picked up the cards James had dealt and frowned. Fuck, another bad hand. "Um, Christmas night."

James shook my hand. "That's great, Lucas. I'm really happy. There was always something about the two of you that screamed couple. I'm glad you both finally saw it."

I laughed, then coughed.

"What's so funny?" James asked.

Looking around the table, Shawn said, "You didn't know? Hell, Hollie put a damn spell on Lucas so he would notice her, but it all went wrong, and she actually put a hex on him."

James and Alex both looked at me.

"I didn't know Hollie was into that," Alex stated. "I need to let Mary know. She's really been into crystals and shit lately. We've been trying to have a baby, and she's doing everything she can think of. She even gets on her head after we have sex sometimes. It's fucking weird, but I love her, so I get on my head next to her."

I was positive we were all staring at Alex with confused looks. "Why in the hell are you getting on your head too?" Shawn asked.

Alex discarded two cards and picked up two new ones. "I don't know. I feel bad she's doing it, so I do it with her. I just want her to be happy, ya know?" Alex said with a shy grin. "I'll do whatever I have to do to make her happy, and if that's standing on my head, then so be it."

I couldn't help but smile. James nodded, and Shawn grunted in mock disgust. He could act like he wasn't wanting a relationship all he wanted, but I had a feeling he was ready to settle down. And if my girlfriend had anything to say about it, it would be sooner rather than later.

"Fuck that. No woman is ever going to make me jump through hoops for them. Hell would freeze over before that happens," Shawn said.

Glancing at the time, I was guessing it was either too early for the spell, or Hollie changed her mind. I was hoping it was the latter. The last thing any of us needed was a woman who just found out she had the power to play cupid with spells.

"You say that now, Shawn," Alex said as he tossed in more money, "but someday, the right woman is going to come along and turn your world upside down."

Something passed over my best friend's face, and I decided to investigate Hollie's claims.

"What about Kristin?" I asked.

Shawn's head jerked up so fast, I thought for sure he was going to strain something from the movement. "Kristin?"

"Yeah."

"Kristin who?" James asked.

"Kristin Mills," I answered.

Alex laughed. "Kristin Mills? Damn, she was fucking hot in high school. James, didn't you try to get into her pants a few times?"

I watched Shawn as he turned his attention on James, a look of anger moving over his face.

"Sure as shit did," James said as he stared at his cards. "Tried my moves on her a few nights ago when I saw her at a company holiday party."

"You hit on Kristin?" Shawn asked, his voice sounding a little too angry. I raised a brow, but he ignored me.

Not hearing the threatening tone in Shawn's voice, James nodded, then tossed in some money. "Yeah. Didn't get anywhere with her, though."

Shawn seemed to relax a little.

"One of the other lawyers I work with seemed to make a better impression on her, though. I think he said he's taking her out to dinner tomorrow night."

And that was when I saw it. Jealousy mixed with anger. He tried to hide it, but I had been watching him. Holy shit. Hollie was right. Shawn nearly crumbled the cards in his hand. He set them down and got up. "Beer?" he asked as he headed toward his kitchen.

"I'll take one," James and Alex both said.

Standing, I glanced down at the bowl of chips and another bowl of pretzels. I knew I should have eaten before I came over. "I'm going to see if he has any real food. Don't look at my cards."

The bastards both laughed as I got up and shot them each a dirty look.

I found Shawn standing with his hands on the counter, his head bent.

"Want to talk about it?" I asked.

He spun around and forced a smile. "Talk about what?"

"Why you're in the kitchen trying to calm down."

Leaning back onto the counter, he crossed his ankles and attempted to look casual. "I'm not doing that at all."

"Really? Because I saw the way your face nearly turned to stone at the mention of someone taking Kristin out."

He exhaled and ran his hand through his hair. "It's just, the woman drives me fucking crazy, Lucas. She argues with me about everything. This whole engagement surprise thing you asked us to help you with... It's her way or no way."

"I can ask her to back off some."

He shook his head. "No, no, don't do that. Hollie is her best friend, and no one knows her any better besides you. Her ideas are good, and I know they're coming from the heart."

"Then what's the problem?" I asked.

Closing his eyes, he appeared to be debating what to say.

"That time we slept together, I thought I was doing the right thing by leaving. I thought she was just interested in a one-time thing. I mean, I wanted more from her, but she wasn't making it seem like that was something she wanted as well." He pushed his hand through his hair. "Why are women so complicated?"

"Not sure," I answered.

"I left when she fell asleep, and I'm positive that's why she's so pissed off. Instead of talking to me about it, she puts up this wall and turns into a royal bitch."

"Did you tell her you were leaving?"

The look in his eyes told me he hadn't.

"Damn, dude, she thinks you ghosted her. No wonder she's pissed."

"I didn't know what to do. It was different with her, and if she wasn't feeling the same as me... I don't know. I can't explain it."

Frowning, I asked, "What do you mean, it was different with her?"

He sighed heavily. "Sex with Kristin was different. It felt different. It wasn't just about a one-time fuck. It felt deeper, and I think a part of me got freaked out by that, so maybe I just put it in my own head that she wasn't returning the vibe. Ever since then, she's been cold to me. I don't blame her."

"Have you ever thought of talking to her about it? Maybe it was different for her as well."

With a shake of his head, he pushed off the counter and opened the refrigerator. He grabbed three beers. "She hates me, Lucas. She's made it abundantly clear she wants nothing to do with me. Why bother telling her now?"

I shrugged. "Because maybe it's a defense mechanism that she is using to keep you away or to keep her own feelings hidden."

"I don't think so."

I was about to tell him what Hollie thought when Alex walked into the kitchen. "What in the hell are you two doing in here? I'm ready to take Dayton's money away from him."

"I'm going to order some pizza," I said as I motioned for the two of them to head on back to the poker table.

When I pulled my phone out of my pocket, I saw I had a text from Hollie.

Hollie: Good luck tonight!

Me: Thanks, I'll need it.

After ordering a few pizzas, I headed back to the poker table where I lost the first two hands.

Chapter Six

Hollie

When Kristin had shown up with the largest bottle of wine I'd ever seen, I knew it was going to be easy to get her to go along with my little plan.

After eating Chinese take-out, I sat us down at the table where I had a little altar set up.

"What spell are we doing tonight?" she asked, rubbing her hands together.

"A good luck spell for Lucas. He's playing poker with Shawn, James, and Alex."

I watched for something on Kristin's face when I mentioned Shawn's name, but it was blank.

"James tried to get into my pants a few weeks back at the holiday party at my father's law firm."

"No way!" I said with a giggle. "What happened?"

"I brushed him off, but somehow, I ended up agreeing to go to dinner with this guy, Martin. Wait, is that his name? Yeah, Martin. My father likes him, and I thought maybe it would earn me some brownie points."

I gave Kristin a sad smile. Her whole life, she had been trying to make her father happy. He always seemed to put her down at any chance he got.

"Okay, so what do we need to do?"

"You want to do the spell with me?" I asked.

"Hell, yes! What did Sarah say? A spell is good with one witch, but a coven of witches makes it stronger."

I giggled. "Okay, we need to write 'money' on the green candle, then write it on this piece of paper. Then under it, write 'luck for poker night.'"

Kristin nodded as she wrote, and I wrote some things myself.

"Now what?" she asked.

"We place the coins on the top of the paper. Four pennies, one quarter, five dimes."

Kristin and I laid out the coins.

Picking up the lighter, I took the green candle. "Hold onto it with me, and really put your emotion into it. Sarah said it's really important."

Nodding, Kristin said, "Got it."

"Now, we have to say seven times, 'Like the trees growing free, luck for Lucas shall be.'"

"Really? Can't we come up with a cuter rhyme than that?"

Shooting her a warning look, I said, "It's not a rhyme, it's a spell!"

"Is that really the spell?" she asked with one brow raised.

"No, but it's close enough."

"Fine. Let's do this."

As I lit the candle, I nodded for her to speak with me. "Like the trees growing free, luck for Lucas shall be."

We repeated it seven times. I handed the candle to Kristin and folded the paper toward me, turning and folding it until I couldn't fold it anymore. I took a green ribbon and held it up.

"Green for money!" I giggled as Kristin laughed.

"I just need to wrap it around this. Every three rotations, we have to say, 'Money flowing free, prosperity there shall be.' And we have to think of Lucas as we say it. Ready?"

"Ready!"

As I turned the ribbon-wrapped packet, Kristin and I said the chant. I reached for the dragon's blood smudge stick and waved it in the air.

"What's with the smudge stick?" Kristin asked.

"Dragon's blood adds potency to the spells."

She nodded. "Good to know."

"Okay. We just need to let the candle burn down."

Kristin stood. "This calls for more wine."

"How about a whiskey shot?" I asked.

Glancing over her shoulder, she flashed me a wicked grin. "I like where your head is."

After two shots and two glasses of wine, I decided to test the waters.

"Kristin, I want to... No, I want you to put a spell on Shawn."

She looked over at me. "One where his dick falls off? If that's the kind of spell you're talking about, then I'm all for it."

I rolled my eyes. "Why do you hate him so much?"

Placing her wine on the table, Kristin leaned forward, causing me to do the same as I waited for her to finally tell me what her beef was with Shawn.

"We slept together a few years back, and he left in the middle of the night. No goodbye, no nothing. Just left."

My mouth fell open. "You slept with Shawn?"

"No, I had an evening of the best sex of my life with a man I haven't been able to stop thinking about or comparing every guy I'm with to. He's ruined my sex life forever!"

My hand came up to my mouth, and I fought to hold back a laugh. "Wow. It was that good, huh?"

She closed her eyes. "The man can do things with his tongue…"

"Ewww! Gross! I don't want to hear that."

With a half-shoulder shrug, she winked at me.

"Okay, hear me out."

Kristin reached for her wine glass, nearly knocking it over, so I knew she was a bit tipsy but not drunk. Yet.

"Why do I feel like I'm not going to want to hear you out?"

"The spell that we thought we were doing on Lucas, the notice me spell…? Well, I've got the right spell now."

Okay, so I wasn't exactly telling her it was a charm spell. She'd forgive me.

"So?"

"So!" I said as I attempted to act excited. "Let's use it on Shawn!"

She stared at me for a few minutes before she busted out laughing.

"What's so funny?" I asked as I folded my arms over my chest.

"The difference is, you wanted Lucas to notice you. I could care less if Shawn knows I'm in the same room with him or not."

Tilting my head, I gave her a look that said, *Really?*

"Kristin, I'm your best friend. You don't think I've noticed the way you look at him when you think no one is watching. And the way he looks at you! He wants you."

She looked up from the wine glass that was pressed to her lips. "You think so?"

Oh, my gosh. I'm pulling her in! Internal fist bump for me!

"I don't think so, I know so!"

She put her wine glass down. "You think he...wants me?"

"For sure. It's written all over his face. And I get this weird feeling when you two are together. And who knows what that means? I don't fully understand all these witch powers yet, but I'm thinking it's a force between you two. You said the sex was good."

"It was more than good," she said, dropping back and pulling her legs up under her. "It was hot. It was passionate. It was...sweet."

"Then let's do this!" I ran to the kitchen and grabbed the white sage and lavender smudge. "Look! I bought this at Lucy's today. White sage and lavender are thought to spark passion. They're an aphrodisiac and also happen to promote a deep relaxation."

"Wait, do you think we should use that? I mean, I just want him to notice me.... No, I want him to notice me and realize what he lost!"

I chewed on my lip. That wasn't exactly where I wanted her to go with her thoughts. "You don't want him again?"

"Sex-wise? Hell, I'd take another go in the sheets with him. Show him what he's missed out on."

Studying her face, I knew she was lying. She wanted more than sex.

"Then are you down for doing the spell?"

She drew in a deep breath, held it, then exhaled. "Why the fuck not! I'm halfway to drunk, so what the hell?"

Jumping up, I clapped my hands. "I'll get it all set up! Here, have another shot and more wine!"

After gathering everything up, I made my way back into the living room. For a moment, I paused as I thought about the night we cast a spell on Lucas. A moment of panic hit me, but I brushed it away.

"I've got this," I said as I pulled the dining room chair into the room. "Okay, sit here and think about Shawn."

Kristin's eyes were glossy, and her cheeks were slightly red. "Got it!" she said with a salute.

She sat down in the chair, and I lit the white sage and lavender smudge stick, then moved it around the room.

"That smells good!"

"Shh! Think about Shawn!"

"Right! Shawn. Thinking about him now."

I moved around the room and said, "Picture you and Shawn together."

"Sexually?"

Rolling my eyes, I replied, "However you want!"

She smiled, and I curled my lip as she licked her lips. "Anyway, think about the two of you together. Now, take this red candle."

Kristin opened her eyes and reached for the red candle. I handed her a knife. "Carve his name in the candle."

"Okey dokey!"

Two seconds later, Kristin yelped. "I cut myself."

"Damn it, Kristin!"

She giggled. "Well, we should have done this when I was sober!"

"If I thought you would have, we would have!"

Her brows pulled down. "What?"

I took her hand and helped her carve his name.

"Oh, wait, maybe we were supposed to carve your name?"

Kristin started laughing.

"Let's put your name on the other side! Couldn't hurt to have both names."

"No, not at all. What could possibly go wrong?!" she said between a hiccup and a laugh.

"Now we need to inscribe, 'bring love.'"

"Or hot sex. Let's put hot sex instead."

Ignoring her, I held her hand and attempted to carve in "bring love."

"I still think we should put hot sex."

I couldn't help it. I giggled. "Okay! I'll carve it in!"

Another round of giggles hit Kristin as she reached for her wine and the smudge stick that she started waving all over.

"Put that down and place the candle in the middle of this plate."

It took Kristin a few times to get the candle in the little holder on the plate, but she finally got it.

"Okay. Now you need to take the cloves, nutmeg, and sugar and mix them in this bowl with intent."

"Contempt? Why?"

"No, not contempt, *intent*. Like you intend on having hot passionate sex with Shawn because he's going to want that!"

"*Yes!*" Kristin said as she mixed the spices. She wore a deep, concentrated expression, and I nodded.

"Good! Good! Now you have to sprinkle the mixture in a circle around the candle, and you have to say seven times, '*In your mind, you will see only me. If love is to be, your will shall be free.*'"

She scrunched up her face. "That's a lot to say. Can you write it down so I can read it?"

I handed her the piece of paper. "Can you sprinkle and read at the same time?"

"Hold on...wench. Let me read it a few times. I'm not *that* drunk. I can remember it."

As I waited for Kristin to learn the spell, I tapped my fingers on my knees.

"Okay. Got it!"

"Great. I'll hold the bowl for you and the paper if you need to read it."

She nodded as she reached into the bowl and took some of the spices.

"In your mind, you will see me. If love is to be, your will shall be free."

I nodded and motioned for her to say it again. She said it five more times, then changed it up on the last one.

"In your mind, you will see me naked and you inside me. If your love is to be, you will set yourself free in me!"

"Gross, Kristin!" I gagged, then shook the paper. "Say it the right way."

Somehow between her laughing, me giggling, and spices going everywhere, she managed to say the spell.

"Now what?" Kristin asked as she sat back in the chair.

"You're supposed to see yourself with him as the candle burns down."

She nodded. "Want to play dirty-word Scrabble while we wait?"

"Ohh! That sounds like fun!"

Chapter Seven

Lucas

Alex stared at me as he waited for me to show my cards. I laid them out, and Alex cursed.

"Royal flush, baby!" I said as I pulled the pile of chips over to me.

"What the fuck? That's the last five hands you won. I'm done. I have no more money left," Alex stated as he attempted not to pout.

I looked at James and Shawn. "Are you also going to pull out simply because I've had a round of good luck?"

"I think you're cheating," Shawn accused. "You suck at poker, Lucas. How is it you suddenly became a blank page? I haven't been able to read your face at all. And when you do frown like you have a bad hand, it's a good hand. It's confusing."

Laughing, I said, "I'm sorry, isn't that what poker is all about? Come on, one more hand."

James shook his head. "Nope. I need to walk out of here with my head held high. Losing to you has thrown me."

"Is it hot in here to you guys?" Shawn asked.

Alex gave him a befuddled look. "Hot? No. It feels good."

"It's so hot. I feel like I'm burning up. Do you smell... lavender?"

My eyes jerked up from my winnings. "What?"

"Lavender. I smell lavender."

"Dude, how many beers have you had to drink?" James asked Shawn.

Shawn wiped his forehead. "The same amount as you. Fuck, it's so hot."

"Why don't we step out onto the back porch?" I suggested as I stood up.

"The back porch? It's freaking below freezing out there now, Lucas," Alex said as he stood and placed the back of his hand on Shawn's forehead. "You don't feel hot."

Alex was a registered nurse, so I was confident he would be able to tell whether Shawn was running a fever.

"Do you smell the lavender?" Shawn asked. "It smells like...like her."

James chuckled. "Like who?"

Shawn looked confused as he answered, "Kristin. It smells like her."

"Oh, hell," I mumbled.

James and Alex both looked at me and said at the same time, "What is he talking about?"

"Listen, guys, I think we should wrap up poker night. I think Shawn's had a little more to drink than we thought."

James nodded and pulled out some money for my winnings. Alex did the same but kept looking at Shawn who was now pacing.

Alex handed me some money and narrowed his eyes. "You didn't cheat?"

I laughed. "I swear, I didn't cheat."

He pushed the money into my hand, then looked back at Shawn. "Is he okay?"

"Yeah," I said as I started toward the door, hoping James and Alex would follow. "He just needs to get some sleep, I think."

"Better give him some Advil before he goes to sleep if he drank too much."

I squeezed Alex's shoulder. "Will do. This was fun!"

Alex curled his lip up at me. "I would say beginner's luck, but since we've been playing for ten years, I can't."

Laughing, I practically pushed them both out the door. "Night, guys! Talk soon and thanks for your money."

They both shot me the finger as they walked down the steps as snow fell around them. Shutting the door, I spun around and quickly made my way back to the living room. I pulled out my phone and was about to call Hollie when I ran into Shawn. He had his jacket on and his keys in his hand.

"Where do you think you're going?"

"I need to get to Kristin. I need to see her."

"Right now?" I asked with a humorless laugh. "Dude, it's nearly one in the morning, and you've been drinking."

He scrubbed his hands down his face. "I don't know what's wrong with me, but I...I...I need to see her. I need to touch her. Feel her. Be with her."

Holy hell, Hollie, what did you do?

"Listen to me, Shawn. You don't need to do any of those things. I think this is all Hollie."

He shook his head. "No, I've been fighting this attraction, and I can't do it any longer. I need to see her, Lucas. Now."

"Okay, listen. It's the middle of the night, Shawn. Just sleep this off and see how you feel in the morning. Okay?"

He narrowed his eyes but finally nodded. "Fine. I'm feeling kind of exhausted suddenly."

For a moment, I wondered if I also had powers because I had wished for him to pass the hell out.

"Sleep sounds great. You go get ready for bed, and I'll clean up in here." I paused for a moment. Why had I just sounded like my mother? I shivered and pushed the thought away.

He went to walk toward his bedroom, then turned to me. "Your money."

I waved it off. "Pay me later. Go take a cold shower or something."

Shawn nodded, then walked like a damn zombie to his bedroom. I pulled out my phone and called Hollie. It went to voicemail. She must have already been asleep.

When I heard the beep, I quietly said, "Hollie! What did you do? Shawn is acting weird. He keeps saying he's hot and he needs to be with Kristin. He needs to touch her! What the heck is that?"

I heard a bang and quickly made my way to Shawn's room. I could hear the shower going as I walked up to the door and was about to knock to see if he was okay when I heard moaning.

"No...no, no, no," I whispered.

Then Shawn started to call out Kristin's name.

I stumbled back, tripped on something, stumbled to get myself right, then fell right on my ass.

Still able to hear Shawn calling out and moaning, I jumped up.

"Oh, my God! My ears! My ears!" I cried out as I rushed out of the bedroom and back to the dining room. "Oh, my God. I think I just heard my best friend jacking off in the shower!"

I pulled the phone away from my ear. "I just left that on a voicemail!"

Hitting End, I grabbed my jacket, keys, and a piece of cold pizza before I called out, "I'm heading home, Shawn!"

When he didn't reply, I got the hell out of his house, locking the door behind me and praying that Shawn would pass out.

My phone rang as I slipped into my car.

"Hollie!"

"Lucas, what is going on? I heard you screaming 'My ears,' and I think you said you saw Shawn jacking off."

"*No!* No, Hollie, I did not say that! I heard him. *Heard him!* I heard him jacking off. Two very different things!"

"Okay, but why were you in the bathroom while he was–?"

"Do not say it! Please, for the love of everything holy, I need to forget the last few minutes of my life."

"Are you going to at least tell me why you were in the bathroom with him?"

"I wasn't! I heard a noise, went up to check on him, and heard him in the shower. This is all your fault! And I suppose me winning at poker tonight was your doing as well."

"You won! How much did you win?"

I sighed, then turned my car on. "Does it matter? Hollie, whatever you did tonight to Shawn, he is acting like a crazy man. I had to stop him from leaving his house. He wanted to go find Kristin. He said he had to...touch her."

She gasped. "Oh, dear. Oh, okay. Well...um...wow."

"Yeah, my thoughts exactly."

"Maybe we shouldn't have used the smudge stick. I'm sure what Kristin said during the spell didn't help either."

Shaking my head, I counted to ten and chanted in my head, *She's a new witch. She's a new witch.*

"What spell did you put on him?"

Hollie paused for a moment. "It was a simple notice me spell, but I think we might have tweaked it a bit."

"You think you might have? Did you not learn your lesson the first time?!"

"Don't yell at me, Lucas Dayton!"

I drew in a deep breath. "I'm sorry. Okay, let's start over. Whatever you did seems to have made Shawn obsessed with Kristin."

"Define obsessed."

"I'm tired, it's late, it's snowing. I'll talk to you when I get home. Is Kristin still there?"

"Yes, she's sort of passed out on the sofa."

With a tired exhale, I said, "I'll be home soon."

"Be careful. Lucas?"

"Yeah?"

"I love you."

"I love you more, babe."

Chapter Eight

Hollie

I jumped off the sofa when I heard the front door open. Lucas appeared and glanced over at Kristin.

"Is she passed out?" he softly asked.

"No, she was tipsy but not that drunk. She's just sleeping. Let me cover her up, and I'll meet you in the bedroom."

Lucas let out a long, exhausted sigh before he turned and headed toward my bedroom that we both now shared. We seemed to split our time between both of our places.

As I covered up Kristin, she mumbled a thank you and let out a snore. Smiling, I whispered, "You're welcome."

Making my way out of the living room, a sudden thought came to me. I should have a cat. Shouldn't all witches have cats? Shaking off the thought, I hurried to the bedroom and heard the shower going. Locking the bedroom door, I quickly slipped out of my sweats and joined Lucas in the shower.

The feel of the hot water hitting my skin caused me to let out a moan of pleasure before I pressed my body against his back.

"You feel so good," he said as he turned and looked down at me.

"So do you," I replied, returning his grin with one of my own. "Are you mad at me?"

He leaned down and brushed his lips softly over mine. "No, but I think we have a problem."

I flinched. "How big of a problem?"

Lucas lifted me up, and I wrapped my legs around his body. "We can talk after I fuck you."

That familiar, delicious pull in my lower stomach had me so ready for Lucas to push inside of me that I pushed my hips against him, silently begging him.

"Are you ready for me?" he asked in a low, growly voice.

My breath came faster, and I answered with, "I'm always ready for you. We have to be quiet, though. Kristin, remember?"

He reached down and lined himself up with my entrance, then thrust inside of me, causing me to gasp from the sudden fullness, then moan with the heavenly feel of him.

"I can't do slow tonight, Hollie."

I dug my fingers into his hair and pulled his head back. With my lips hovering over his, I whispered, "I don't want slow."

Lucas began to move inside me fast and hard, and I knew it wasn't going to take long for me to explode. I could feel it building, and I was just on the cusp of it.

"Oh, God, I'm so close," I panted out in a whispered voice.

"Fuck, yes," Lucas hissed as he pulled out and slammed back into me. My back was pressed against the cold shower wall, and the feel of it, plus the heat from the sex was winding me up so tight, I knew it was going to be one hell of an orgasm.

"Lucas, don't stop."

"Never," he said before he pressed his mouth to mine. His hands cupped my cheeks tightly, and his finger moved and pressed against what I referred to as "the no-go zone," slowly slipping inside and sending me hurdling off the ledge.

"Oh, my God!" I cried out before his mouth was capturing my screams of pleasure. Jesus, Mary, and all of the saints above, this had to be the best orgasm of my life or close to it.

Lucas moved faster, harder, and I could feel him growing inside me. He moaned into my mouth and came inside of me as I attempted to come down from my own mind-blowing orgasm.

When he finally stilled, I felt my body go limp. "I'm spent," I whispered.

Lucas chuckled and gently lifted me up so he could pull out of me, then lowered me until my feet hit the floor of the shower. I dropped my head back against the cool tile, and I let out a contented sigh.

"Did that feel good?" he asked, his mouth placing kisses along my jaw and neck.

"You slipped your finger into the no-go zone."

I could feel him smile against my skin. "Did it not feel good?"

"It felt freaking fantastic. I've never felt an orgasm like that before."

He drew his head back and looked down at me with a devilish smile. "So, we liked the butt play?"

I felt my cheeks heat with embarrassment.

"Don't do that. Don't be embarrassed for feeling good, Hollie."

Biting down on my lower lip, I stared at his chest as I answered him. "I mean, I don't know how far I want to go, but it did feel good when you slipped your finger inside."

He nuzzled my neck. "It was so fucking hot, I want to do it again."

I wrapped my arms around his neck. "I'm down for that, but remember, we have a guest."

And that was when his body went from completely relaxed to tense. He stepped away, and I instantly missed the heat of his body. I followed and stood under the shower.

"We need to talk."

"Okay," I softly said. "Now or in the morning?"

Lucas took the soap and started to move it over my body. I wanted to moan when his hands went over my breasts, but I forced myself not to.

"After the shower. Turn around," he commanded.

Doing as he said, I leaned against his body as he pulled me to him. His soapy hand moved between my legs and lifted one up and propped it against the seat in the shower. It only took him rubbing my clit a few times, and I was pressing my hand over my mouth and coming once again. His arm tightened around my waist as my entire body felt like it was going to melt to the ground.

"Let's finish up in here. I'm exhausted, and I want to hold you while I fall asleep."

Turning, I rinsed off and then watched as he quickly soaped himself up. We both got out of the shower and dried off. After we each slipped on some pajamas, we crawled up into the bed, and I braced myself for what was going to come next. Instead of letting him just go for it, I spoke first.

"I'm sorry for the spell I put on you for the good luck. I just really wanted you to win a hand or two."

He laughed. "I won them all after losing the first few. I'm not mad, but if the guys find out, they'll accuse me of cheating. It was just for tonight, right?"

I nodded. "We'll keep it between us."

He winked and my stomach flipped. How could my body want him again? I was the one obsessed, it seemed.

"We do have to talk about the spell you put on Shawn."

Shaking my head, I replied, "I didn't put the spell on him. Kristin did."

He frowned. "Is she a witch too?"

"All of us have a little witch in us. I think, by helping her with the spell, I might have made it a bit stronger. Sarah mentioned that when I put the spell on you. Something about a spell being strong when a coven of witches performed it. But a small part of me thinks Kristin might have the gift. Anyway, I used a smudge stick as well. A white sage and lavender, and that is known to boost the potency of the spell as well as spark passion. It's also an aphrodisiac."

Lucas ran his fingers through my hair. "That explains his need to get to Kristin. But it seemed more...sexual."

"That," I said with conviction, "I blame on Kristin. I gave her the spell to say, and she had to repeat it seven times. The last time, she changed it."

He looked weary but asked, "To what?"

"Well," I began as I twisted my hands in my lap, "at the time, I thought it was kind of funny, but now I'm thinking it wasn't."

Closing his eyes, he asked, "What did she say?"

"She was only supposed to say, 'In your mind, you will see me,' but instead she said, 'In your mind, you will see me naked and inside me.'"

Lucas gagged. "I didn't need that visual."

"Right? That's what I was saying. Gross! Anyway, I honestly didn't think anything of it."

"Considering all Shawn wanted to do was get to Kristin—hold her, touch her—yeah, I'm pretty sure that was what he was seeing. And then the moment that shall not be named happened."

I pressed my mouth together in a tight line so I wouldn't laugh.

He shook his head. "What's going to happen when he finally sees her? He wouldn't...force her, would he?"

"No!" I quickly said. "Of course not. I mean, I don't honestly know what he's going to do, but I don't think it will be anything like that. He may just be infatuated with her."

Lucas frowned but nodded. "Okay, that might not be so bad."

"And if he is paying her attention like that, then Kristin will give him the attention he needs, and all will be perfect! Everyone will be holly jolly for Christmas!"

He shot me a look that said he really didn't believe it would be that simple, and I reached for his hand. "Let's just see what happens. If something went wrong, then..."

My voice trailed off as I thought about what I was going to have to do. Ask either Sarah, Lucy, or my mom for help.

"If Kristin has to do a spell to reverse the first one, like you did, she is going to be so pissed," Lucas warned.

A sudden chill filled the air, and I scrunched up my face. "I know. Let's just hope it doesn't come to that."

The sound of the doorbell ringing caused me to sit straight up in the bed. A sudden déjà vu hit me, and I threw the covers off and jumped out of bed.

"I'm going to kill whoever that is," Lucas mumbled as he rolled over and slowly sat up.

"It's Sarah," I told him.

Scrubbing his hands over his face, he asked, "How do you know?"

"Just call it a hunch."

After slipping on my slippers and robe, I rushed to the living room and saw that Kristin was long gone. When had she left?

Opening the door, I was about to start to explain when I clamped my mouth shut and stared at the man standing in front of me.

"Shawn?"

"Hey, Hollie. Is Kristin around?"

"Oh. Dear. God."

He narrowed his eyes. "I'm sorry?"

"Why would you think she was here?" I asked as I attempted not to freak out. I looked past him and didn't see Sarah. Strange, I had such a strong feeling it was her.

"Didn't you guys have a girls' night last night? I texted her late last night, and she said she was crashing at your house."

I studied Shawn. He seemed normal. Not sex-crazed or in need of finding Kristin right away. Maybe he had to talk to her about her taxes again?

"Why did you need to talk to her?"

His cheeks turned red, and he rubbed at the back of his neck. "I um, I've just been thinking about her and wanted to see her. Talk to her."

Okay. Stay calm, Hollie. He only wants to talk to her. That means he's noticed her in a different way. That was good.

"About her taxes?" I asked.

Shawn laughed. "Why would I want to talk to her about her taxes?"

That caused me to narrow my gaze at him suspiciously. "Aren't you helping her with them? That's why you guys were at lunch together about, wasn't it?"

He looked confused for a moment before he snapped his fingers and pointed to me. "Yes. We were. Talking about taxes and stuff. This is more...um...personal."

"Hey, Shawn. What brings you by so early?" Lucas asked in a dry tone as he shot me a look that said he knew exactly why his best friend was there.

Shawn looked past me and smiled when he saw Lucas. "Just seeing if Kristin was here."

I shook my head as I looked at the empty spot on the sofa. "She's not. She left earlier and I'm not sure where she went."

A look of disappointment crossed his face, and for a moment, I felt sorry for him.

"I'm assuming Hollie has invited you in for coffee."

I jumped. "Oh, right! Sorry, come on in."

Shawn followed us to the kitchen and slid onto one of the stools at my small kitchen island bar.

"I never did pay you for your winnings last night," Shawn stated as Lucas shot me another look.

"Don't worry about it, dude, it was winners' luck," Lucas deadpanned.

I gave a tight smile and quickly got to work making some coffee.

"What do you have planned for today, Shawn?" I asked as I placed a coffee mug in front of him.

He gave me a warm smile. "I'm not sure."

Before he could go on, the front door opened, and I heard Kristin's cheerful, and slightly annoying, morning greeting.

"Good morning! Good morning! Good morrrrrning!"

She came to an abrupt halt when she saw us all in the kitchen.

Shawn jumped up, a wide grin on his face. "Kristin!"

At the same time, Kristin curled her lip up at Shawn and drawled out, "Shawn."

When she saw his reaction to her, she looked confused.

Shawn made his way over to her. He took the box of donuts and coffee out of her hands, then took her hands in his. "I tried calling you."

Kristin's mouth dropped, and she looked at her hands clasped in Shawn's, then back up at him.

"I, um, I haven't checked my voicemail."

"It's okay. I was wondering what you were doing today. I thought maybe we could spend the day together."

Kristin opened her mouth, closed it, then opened it again before asking, "You want to spend the day with me?"

The next thing I knew, Shawn pulled her to him, cupped her face, and kissed her. Not a sweet, peck-on-the-lips kind of kiss. Oh, no, it was a passionate kiss. A heated kiss.

"Oh. My. God." I whispered.

Lucas leaned in to softly say against my ear, "You don't know the strength of your own powers, Hollie."

Smiling, I watched as Kristin melted into Shawn's embrace. "Apparently not, but look at that kiss!"

Shawn drew back and Kristin seemed to sway for a moment before her eyes snapped open.

"I've been thinking about kissing you all night and all morning," Shawn confessed.

"You...you have?" Kristin stammered as her eyes shot over to me, then back to Shawn.

"Tell me you'll spend the day with me. I need to be near you. Then maybe you could stay the night with me."

"Wh-what? Stay the night as in at your house?"

Shawn nodded and took a step closer to Kristin. "I can't deny my feelings anymore. I need you, Kristin. I need to feel your bare skin against mine again."

"And he just lost his man card," Lucas whispered.

Elbowing him in the ribs, I gave him a stern look. "It's the spell talking."

"The spell that went wrong!" he whisper-shouted back.

"Wait, what?" Kristin asked as her head snapped back over to look at me. She narrowed one eye and then slowly shook her head.

I instinctively took a step back but bumped into Lucas who gave me a little push forward. Sold out by the love of my life. I was going to remember that.

Kristin looked at Shawn, smiled, then turned to glare at me as she said, "Hollie, we need to talk. In private."

Pointing to the box from the bakery, I quickly said, "But the coffee is ready, and look, you brought goodies. We should all eat!"

Kristin walked up and grabbed my arm. "Now!"

"I'll come with you," Shawn said as he rushed to stand next to Kristin.

She seemed so discombobulated, I couldn't help but giggle, which earned me a pinch on the back of my arm.

"Ouch!"

"It's girl stuff. Private girl stuff."

Shawn nodded. "But you're not leaving, right?"

Kristin stared at him for a moment, then forced a smile. "Nope. I'll be right back."

She nearly pulled my arm out of the socket as she dragged me through the house and to the guest bedroom. Once the door shut, she leaned against it, her hand on her chest as she drew in a few deep breaths.

"Are you okay?" I asked.

"He kissed me."

"I saw," I said with a giggle. "Looked like a pretty intense kiss."

She lifted her head and gave me a blank expression before her face turned red. "What did you do!?"

"Excuse me, but you did it. You did the spell."

"After you got me tipsy! And you said it was just a notice me spell."

I scrunched up my face and gave a light-hearted laugh. "Well, considering how the last one went..."

"Hollie!" Kristin said as she pushed away from the door and started to pace.

"I'm sorry! I'm sorry! I think it was a few things that messed it up," I said as I turned and watched her as she walked and worried her hands.

"Like doing the spell when I told you not to."

Kristin and I both spun around to find my sister, Sarah, standing in the doorway. She shut the door and gave me that look only an older sister who was disappointed in you could give.

"Okay, now you show up. I knew you were coming."

Sarah smirked. "I'm sure you did."

"You knew about this?" Kristin asked.

Sarah looked at her and nodded. "She told me she was going to ask you if you wanted to do the spell."

"I did!" I stated.

Sarah looked confused for a moment. Then she walked over and sat on the edge of the bed. "Tell me everything you did."

Kristin rushed over and dropped to the floor in front of Sarah. "You have to fix this, Sarah! Your sister did something that made Shawn do more than notice me! He said he wanted to feel my bare skin against his! He kissed me!"

"He kissed you?" Sarah asked. "Was it a good kiss?"

Kristin's head pulled back in shock. "Well, um, yeah, it was really good."

"You enjoyed it? Welcomed it?"

"Well, of course, I did. I've been..."

Her voice trailed off, and I quickly made my way over to her. "You've been what?"

"Nothing," Kristin replied.

Sarah's face erupted in a smile. "You've been wanting him to notice you, to kiss you. And he must have been wanting the same thing for the spell to have worked like it did."

I cleared my throat. "Well, we might have changed one or two things."

Sarah's smile faded as she closed her eyes, appeared to count to ten, then looked directly at me. "Tell me what you did."

"Okay, well, everything was fine until Kristin changed the last part of the spell and said something about wanting Shawn to see her naked and be inside her, or something like that."

Sarah looked at Kristin who simply shrugged. "I was tipsy and slightly horny."

Pinching her brows, Sarah whispered, "It's only nine in the morning, and I need a drink."

"Same," Kristin and I both said.

"Oh, and I used a white sage and lavender smudge during the spell."

With a long, exasperated sigh, Sarah stood. "You only made the spell stronger by doing that."

"I think so because Lucas said Shawn was desperate to get to Kristin last night, and he heard him jerking off in the shower and calling out Kristin's name."

Sarah gagged while Kristin's eyes went wide.

"He did? He was masturbating while thinking of me?" Kristin asked with her hand over her heart. "Oh, my gosh! Last night, I did the same th—"

Sarah covered Kristin's mouth. "Don't. Say. It. Please, I don't need another visual."

My hand came up to my mouth to contain my laughter.

Sarah started to pace the room and mumbled something I wasn't entirely too sure I wanted to hear. She suddenly stopped and looked at both of us.

"You two clearly need to not do spells together. And Kristin, I'm seriously thinking you may be a witch as well. We'll need to look at your family tree."

Kristin jumped as she clapped. "Oh, my gosh! Do you think so?"

I rolled my eyes. "As you were saying, Sarah…"

"Kristin, by you doing the spell in the…state…you were in, you passed off your…" She cleared her throat. "…horny vibes over to Shawn. The only way you could have done that is if you had a lot of magick going into the spell."

"That's why you think she might be a witch?" I asked.

Sarah nodded. "We all have some kind of power in us, it's just knowing how to use it. Some have it more than others."

"My mother used to always tell me we all had a little witch in us," Kristin said. "I wonder if she was trying to tell me something?"

I smiled at her as she smiled at me.

"Well, as fun as you two think this is, you've messed with another person."

"But you can't mess with free will," I argued.

Sarah folded her arms and waited for me to piece it together. I hated teachable moments.

Then it hit me. "Oh, my God. Shawn has feelings for Kristin. That's why the spell is so powerful. It simply enhanced his desires."

"Well, that's kind of disappointing. Would he have not kissed me like that had we not altered the spell?"

Sarah shook her head. "I'm sure he would have. It's just now, he is being very open about his feelings. He can't stop himself."

"How do we get him to go back to being normal?" I asked.

"Wait!" Kristin said as she stepped between us. "I don't want to go back to fighting with him all the time. I want...I want to see where things will go with us."

Sarah took Kristin's hand. "The only way to do that, Kristin, is to remove the spell and go about it the old-fashioned way. Don't you want to know that he wants you because of how he feels and not because you put a spell on him?"

Tears formed in Kristin's eyes as she nodded. I wrapped my arm around her as she dropped to a seated position on the bed.

"What do we have to do?" I asked.

"The reversal spell, but Kristin must be the one to do it. That means, you have to tell him about the spell."

Kristin chewed on her lip. "He's going to be so mad."

I took her hand in mine. "Maybe not. He might think it's funny, and it will bring you guys together like it did me and Lucas."

Kristin nodded, then looked up at Sarah. "Okay, so if I have to turn him back to the grumpy jerk he was before, can I not just enjoy today with him like this? I mean, the sex would probably be amazing."

Sarah, who had sat down on the other side of Kristin, dropped back onto the bed and let out a frustrated cry that I was pretty sure woke the undead.

Chapter Nine

Lucas

"What are they doing?" Shawn asked as he looked in the direction the girls had gone.

"Talking."

He shot me a dirty look. "I know that, but about what? And fuck, why am I lusting after Kristin like this? Did you see me kiss her? I just up and kissed her. And she kissed me back!"

I drew in a long breath and slowly exhaled. I wasn't sure what Hollie and Kristin were up to, but I was going to give it to my boy straight.

"I don't know how to tell you this, Shawn, but last night, Hollie talked Kristin into putting a spell on you."

His brows drew down. "What do you mean?" he asked as he looked back once again through the doorway.

"Look at you, man! Have you ever lusted after Kristin like this?"

Shawn looked back at me. "Yes, but I wasn't so open about it. What in the hell is happening? Do you know how many times I jerked myself off last night and this morning thinking about her? I feel like I'm losing my mind."

Walking over to my best friend, I took him by the shoulders, gave him a good shake, and said, "You're under a spell, man! A spell. They tried to do the notice me spell like what Hollie tried on me, and it went wrong! It, like, made you lust after Kristin."

He blinked a few times at me. "Are you fucking with me?"

"Think about it, Shawn. Think, man. Look past the desire to sleep with Kristin and think!"

Shawn stood, his mouth in a tight, concentrated line. He walked a few feet, turned, and walked back toward me. He did that a few more times before he finally stopped.

"She put a damn spell on me?"

"Yes! I told Hollie not to do it, but she thought she could. Apparently, during the spell, Kristin changed one of the sentences to say something like she wanted you to want to see her naked and...you know."

He narrowed his gaze. "No, I don't know."

"Don't make me say it, dude."

Folding his arms over his chest, he raised a brow.

"Fine. She wanted you to see her naked and inside her." My entire body shivered, and I gagged. "Ugh. I can't believe I had to say that."

A slow smile spread over Shawn's face, and I could see a version of him, before the spell, appearing. "So, now that the spell has gone wrong, what will they need to do?"

"Well, since I saw Sarah breeze through here a few seconds ago, I'm going to guess she is here to help them fix it. Hollie had to do a reversal spell on me, so I'm guessing Kristin will have to do one on you."

"Really?" Shawn asked. "And what if this reversal spell doesn't work?"

I shrugged. "If she does it right, it should. I mean, it worked on me, and I was doubtful."

Shawn scrubbed a hand down his face. "Shit, this is annoying. This constant desire to see the woman!"

"Like I said, spell gone wrong."

"Okay, if that's the game Kristin wants to play, I'll play."

Ah, hell, this can't be good.

"What do you mean by that?"

He leaned against the counter and crossed his ankles. "I'll gladly let her do the reversal spell, but things aren't going to turn out how she thinks."

"Please don't tell me, because the moment you tell me, then I'm going to have to lie to Hollie, and I vowed to never lie to her."

He shrugged. "Then I won't tell you."

"Fine," I said as I picked up a donut and took a bite. It took me all of one minute to break. "Shit. Tell me what your plan is."

A wide grin grew over his face. "If the reversal spell works, I'm going to pretend like it didn't. As a matter of fact, I'm going to kick up the lust factor tenfold."

"This is not going to turn out good, Shawn."

"Oh, I think someone is going to get a taste of her own medicine."

I shook my head, then motioned behind him to let him know the girls were coming back. Kristin looked mad, but the moment she stepped into the kitchen, she focused on Shawn.

"We have to talk."

Shawn pushed off the counter and made his way over to her. Cupping her face once again, he kissed her. I wasn't sure if it was him acting or the damn spell. By the dreamy look on his damn face, I was going with the spell.

"So?" I asked as Hollie walked over to me. She glanced over her shoulder and smiled, then looked back at me. She attempted to wipe the smile away, but I knew she was loving seeing these two idiots together.

"Sarah confirmed what I was thinking. We both think Kristin might have a bit of magick in her own fingertips."

"Oh, Christ," I mumbled.

"The spell was, for sure, more potent, but part of it is because Kristin has real feelings for Shawn, and when we did the spell, she was...you know...the last line and all."

"Yes, yes, I know."

"Sarah said Kristin's feelings kind of, sort of, transferred over to Shawn, and if our suspicions are right, and he has feelings for her too, that just made the spell even more intense. She has to do a..."

Hollie looked back at Shawn and Kristin, and her mouth fell open. "My God, they're practically having sex in our kitchen in front of us! Kristin!"

Kristin quickly broke away from Shawn and placed her hand on her lower stomach. "I need air."

"I can give you everything you need and more," Shawn said as he pulled her back to him.

Kristin pushed him away and held her hand up. "Shawn, I have to tell you something."

"Tell me you want me," he pleaded.

"Tell me he's acting," I mumbled.

Hollie looked at me, "What?"

I shook my head. "Nothing."

Kristin moved to put the kitchen island between her and Shawn.

"I put a spell on you to make you attracted to me, but it was only for you to notice me."

Shawn flashed her what I thought was his sexy smile, or at least that was what the women always said when he smiled like that.

"I've been noticing you, baby. Ever since that night."

Kristin looked stunned. "Really?"

"Kristin," Hollie said in a tone one could only describe as a mom righting her child.

"Right, right," Kristin said as she closed her eyes and shook her head. She focused back on Shawn. "It went all wrong, and now you're obsessed with me and only want to be with me because of the spell. I know neither of us wants that."

Something moved across my best friend's face, but it was gone before I could read it.

"I mean, I want that.... I want you.... No, wait. What I mean is, I want to see where things go between us without a spell."

"But you act like you can't stand me," Shawn said.

Kristin frowned. "Well, you act like you can't stand me."

Shawn slowly let his eyes travel over Kristin and moved toward her. "Let's go back to my place and talk, and maybe some other things. I need to see you..."

"Please don't say naked!" Kristin practically screamed. "That was in the spell, Shawn. You only want that because it was in the spell."

"Shawn, Kristin needs to do a reversal spell on you to stop the spell you're under."

"Wait," Shawn said, clearly missing his calling in life because the bastard was doing a damn good job acting. "Are you telling me you put a spell on me? Like, witchcraft-type shit?"

Kristin and Hollie both nodded.

"You put a spell on me?" he repeated, looking completely devastated. Good God, he was going to deserve an Oscar after this performance. "This feeling I'm feeling...this crazy need to be with you... It's nothing but a spell?"

Kristin started to chew on her thumbnail. "Yes. I'm so sorry, Shawn. I honestly didn't think anything would happen.

I mean, I...I don't know what I was thinking, to be truthful with you. Maybe a small part of me wanted you to notice me for something other than a one-night stand."

And that was where I could see Shawn's entire plan go out the door. "I don't and never have seen you like that, Kristin. I thought that was what you wanted."

"No!" she quickly said. "No, that's not what I wanted. You left in the middle of the night."

"Because I felt something for you, and it scared me that you didn't feel it. I left because I was scared."

Hollie hit me on the side of my arm. "See! I knew this would bring them together! Maybe I should open up a dating site! I could use my powers for good!"

I rolled my eyes. "Let's just stick with the decorating thing, babe."

"So, what do we need to do now?" Shawn asked as he and Kristin both looked at Hollie.

"Are you guys sure you want Hollie helping with this one? I mean, maybe it might be best if we had Sarah help Kristin with the spell."

"Hey!" Hollie said as she stepped in front of me. "I am very capable of helping Kristin reverse the spell! I did yours."

"That's true. She did help you stop hurting yourself."

I shot Kristin a "be quiet" look, then looked down at the hurt expression on Hollie's face. My knees about buckled out from under me. The last thing I would ever want to do was hurt the woman I loved more than the air I breathed.

Focusing back on Hollie, I reached for her hands. "I believe in you, Hollie, and I trust that you know what you're doing. I was kidding."

The corner of her mouth rose in a wobble of a smile. "You really do trust me?"

Leaning down, I kissed her softly. "I really do."

Shawn cleared his throat. "When will we do this reversal spell?"

"Sarah went to Lucy's shop to get everything we need, and she said she'd meet me at your place or mine. Whichever you want. But you're not mad?"

Shawn shook his head and smiled. "Nah. But maybe we can go ahead and go to my place now, and..."

Kristin blushed and looked at Hollie. "See, I told you. The sex would probably be out of this world."

"No, Kristin!" Hollie stated.

Stomping her foot like a child, Kristin looked away. "Fine. Let's go to your place since I think some candle has to stay lit."

"Great! I'll drive," Shawn said as he took Kristin by the hand and nearly dragged her out of the kitchen.

"Should you go with them?" I asked.

Hollie glanced back at where the couple retreated and shook her head. "No. I don't think Kristin will do anything. Sarah had a pretty good talk with her about taking advantage of Shawn when he's under a spell."

I laughed. "Trust me, Shawn is a guy. If he thought for any moment he could sleep with Kristin, spell or no spell, he'd jump at it."

Hollie chewed nervously on her lower lip. "Maybe we should go and stay with them until Sarah brings everything for the reversal."

Nodding, I said, "Let's go get dressed and get over there."

Chapter Ten

Hollie

Lucas and I had gotten to Shawn's house right in time. When we walked in, Shawn was attempting to talk Kristin into going to his bedroom. The moment she saw us, she rushed over and hid behind me.

"When is Sarah going to get here?" she asked.

"She's here," I said only moments before the bell rang.

Lucas looked at me and said, "I wonder if I'll ever get used to that."

I shrugged and winked. "I think it's kind of fun, keeping you on your toes."

Kristin sprinted to the door and opened it. "You're here!" She grabbed Sarah and pulled her into Shawn's living room.

"What do you need me to do?" Kristin and I both asked.

With a pointed look in my direction, Sarah said, "Since you helped her cast the spell, you'll help her uncast it. I've written everything down, and I'll be here should you need any help."

I took the two bags and the paper from Sarah. "Okay. Got it."

"You'll need an altar," Sarah stated.

"I've got a card table in the dining room. We can use that."

"That's perfect, Shawn!" I said as we all followed him to his formal dining room that had been turned into what I was guessing was the poker room.

After Sarah and I got the table ready, Sarah motioned for Lucas to step back from the table.

"Okay, I'll read everything, and you do it, Kristin. Shawn, you just sit down there."

He did as I asked while Kristin put the two bags down on the table.

"First, you'll need a handful of the bay leaves."

"Bay leaves," Kristin said as she took them out of the bag and laid them on the table.

"Next is the Frankincense sticks. A tablespoon of cinnamon powder."

I paused and let Kristin get the cinnamon powder measured out and in the little bowl we had set on the table.

"Okay," Sarah continued. "We have the white candle."

"Got it," Kristin said as Sarah pointed to it. "We also have a dish and a lighter."

"Great!" I said. "That's all we'll need to get started."

"Shawn, you need to empty your mind by taking in three deep breaths," Sarah told him.

I couldn't help but notice Kristin doing the same thing and tried not to smile.

Before I said anything else, I noticed Kristin pick up the lighter and light the white candle. I looked over my shoulder at Sarah who simply raised both brows.

"White candles symbolize clearing paths and invite protection," Kristin stated as I stared at her, my mouth dropped open.

"Shawn, you'll want to put the bay leaves in the middle of the dish." He did as Kristin asked while I watched in utter shock. When Kristin spoke again, I jumped.

"Bay leaves were used in the middle-ages to protect people from plagues and certain types of spells."

Slowly walking backward, I stopped where Sarah and Lucas were and whispered, "What is happening?"

Sarah grinned. "She's finding her magick."

I spun around. "You mean she's a witch, and you knew the whole time?"

Putting her finger up to her mouth, Sarah motioned for me to walk back over to the table. "She might need your guidance. Do you feel the spell coming to you?"

It was then that I realized I had no use for the paper in my hand because I somehow knew the spell.

Kristin pointed to the table as she instructed Shawn. "Now you'll want to sprinkle the cinnamon on top of the leaves."

He did as she asked while she said, "Cinnamon promotes healing and is used in purification rituals."

"I knew that!" Lucas said, causing everyone to look at him. He held up his hands. "Sorry."

"As you add the cinnamon, say after me, 'In the name of the sun, moon, and sky, I invoke the ancient forces.'"

Shawn repeated Kristin's words, and I looked down at the paper, already knowing the spell she spoke was right.

Kristin went on. "To crush and remove all negative spells and crosses."

After Shawn repeated the verse, Kristin said the last one. "Break and dissolve, bless and set free. As it is now, so mote it be."

Shawn repeated her words, and I realized I had been holding my breath the entire time. I slowly exhaled and looked back at Sarah who simply nodded and smiled.

"Now you'll want to take the two incense stickes and cross them over the dish," I explained. "Light them. As they burn, they'll uncross all the negative energies and the spell I put on you. You're going to have to let the candle and sticks burn completely down. All negative influences and spells will start to disappear, and you should start feeling like yourself again."

Shawn nodded.

"Um, if the urges, you know, continue, you can repeat this with new candles and incense sticks for seven days," I added.

"Okay," Shawn simply said. "Do I need to do anything with the candle and sticks once they burn down?"

Kristin looked at me, and I replied, "You'll need to bury them all and as you do, you say, 'thanks.'"

"I say thanks?" Shawn asked with a hint of amusement in his voice.

With a nod, I replied, "Yep."

"How do you feel?" Lucas asked.

Shawn looked around the room. "I mean, I don't have an uncontrolled urge to hump Kristin like a dog, but I wouldn't say no if she wanted me to."

"And that is where I take my leave," Sarah stated as she turned to head toward the front door.

"Sarah! Wait!" Kristin called out as she got up and walked toward my sister. "I knew the spell. How did I know the spell?"

With a wink, Sarah simply said, "Welcome to the coven."

"No! No way," Shawn said. "She's a witch too?"

Spinning on her heels, Kristin flashed Shawn a shit-eating grin as she tapped her fingers together. "Oh, what to do with this new information.... What to do!"

After ordering pizza for lunch, Lucas and I decided to let Kristin and Shawn have some time together. With the way the two of them kept glancing at each other, I was sure the spell was gone, and I wanted them to have privacy to talk.

"Do you think anything will happen between them?" I asked as Lucas pulled away from Shawn's house.

"I think they're both ready to explore that possibility. And I have to say, it was your spell that caused them both to open their eyes and admit their feelings."

"See? I knew it would all turn out okay."

Lucas gave me a *Really?* look.

"Okay, so maybe the first few spells I've tried haven't exactly worked out like I wanted them to, but I'm learning."

He took my hand in his and kissed the back of it. "What do you think about Kristin?"

I moved in my seat to face him some. "Isn't that exciting? And it makes sense why the spell with you turned out like it did. When more than one witch does a spell, it makes it that more powerful."

"And explains what happened to Shawn."

"That too!"

We fell into a comfortable silence before Lucas asked, "You knew Sarah was at the door before she ran the doorbell. Did you see her?"

I shook my head. "More like I sensed her. It's happened to me in the past, but I always ignored it and thought of it as a sixth sense."

"What if someone is planning a surprise, like a birthday party or something? Would you see that ahead of time?"

Thinking about his question, I wondered more about why he was asking it. "No, I don't think so."

He nodded but looked nervous about something. I squeezed his hand. "Hey, is everything okay?"

"Yeah, everything is great."

"Why the questions about seeing things and sensing things?"

He laughed. "I'm just wondering if I'll ever be able to pull off a surprise with you."

Smiling, I replied, "Kristin threw me a surprise birthday party once, and I had no idea. Oh, and one time at work, they threw me an anniversary party, and I was totally clueless. I love surprises, so don't let my weird sixth sense spoil any plans you want to make."

Lucas kissed the back of my hand once again. "I'm glad to hear it, and I won't. Now, can you tell me what I'm thinking right now?"

I closed my eyes tightly and giggled. "You want to pull over somewhere and have sex in your car!"

When he didn't say anything, I sprung my eyes open. "Oh, my gosh, was that what you were thinking?"

He finally laughed. "No, I was thinking we don't have a tree up in my house yet. Should we go get one and decorate it?"

Nearly jumping out of my skin with excitement, I yelled, "Yes! Can we go to Hobby Lobby?"

"Hobby Lobby? Hollie, that's, like, forty minutes away if we go to the one in Seabrook."

Giving him my best pouty look, I said, "Pwease!"

With a roll of his eyes, he answered, "Fine, but you owe me."

I lifted my hand and placed it on his thigh before moving between his legs. "Public sex in the car is still on the table."

Lucas turned and looked at me. "And if we got caught, I'd lose my job, and you'd never get work again."

"How about sex in a random hotel where we check in, make love, then leave. I've always wanted to do that."

Putting on his turn signal, Lucas whipped the car into a parking lot. I looked to see where we were and then laughed my ass off when I saw it was the Marriott Peabody Hotel.

Chapter Eleven

Lucas

"Are you going to say anything, Lucas?" my former college professor, Sam Martin, said as he smiled at me.

"Dr. Martin, I'm a little stunned."

"That I want you to help me on a dig site?"

I blinked at him a few times. "Yes, why me?"

"You have experience in the field, you were one of my top students at Harvard, and I think this would be an amazing opportunity for you. We have stumbled upon a four-thousand-year-old Bronze Age burial site. The things we've already discovered are unbelievable. And there is so much more, Lucas. Isn't this what you wanted when you went to school to become an archaeologist?"

"It was, but I'm happy where I am, Dr. Martin. This past fall, we unearthed a small town that was part of Salem. So far, we've discovered a tavern and lodge, and a small base of a structure we're pretty sure was a church from a few of the recovered artifacts."

Dr. Martin leaned back in his chair and gave me a hard look. "A tavern over a four-thousand-year-old Bronze Age burial site? Lucas, I know you want this. What is holding you back?"

A memory of making love to Hollie this morning popped into my head, and I cleared my throat.

"I see," he said with a slight grin. "How long?"

"I've known her nearly my entire life, been in love with her, I think, for half of that, and it's been official for two months."

He nodded and rubbed his chin. "A new love. I can see why you would be hesitant."

Laughing, I opened my arms and said, "And I have my dream job. I've always wanted this job. I can't walk away from it."

"You can put in a leave of absence and bring your new love with you. I'm sure she'll love the UK."

With a shake of my head, I replied, "I can't do that. She has a life and a very successful career here in Salem. I would never ask her to give up her dream for me to take a job."

"A job?" he barked back. "This is a once-in-a-lifetime opportunity I'm talking about, Lucas. I want you to lead part of the dig. Think of the experience you'll gain. Do you remember when we were in Egypt? How much you loved getting in there and digging? Do you even do any of the work here? I'm almost positive you are overseeing some students, are you not?"

I moved in my chair some. "There are a few, but I have a very knowledgeable staff, and you're wrong. I get in there and dig as well."

He glanced out the window. "In the snow?"

I followed his gaze to see a pretty good snow falling. Hollie would be happy, and the thought made me smile. "No, it's on hold until spring."

"Then you have nothing holding you back, Lucas."

Raising a brow, he waved his hand in front of him. "Women come and go. I've been married five times."

With a humorless laugh, I replied, "I wonder why? You're never home."

He shrugged. "I love my work."

"I do as well, but I love her more."

Dr. Martin stood. "I want you to think about it, okay? Here is my card. It has my updated cell phone number. I'm leaving right after Christmas."

"I've already got a vacation planned with Hollie."

He ignored my comment. "There is a first-class ticket that is yours, leaving for Dublin on December 27. I'm sure you'll make the right decision for your career."

I stood and walked Dr. Martin to the door of my office. Deciding to ignore his last statement, I reached my hand out to shake his. "It was great seeing you again, Dr. Martin. It's been a long time."

"It has. Hopefully, I'll be seeing you soon, Lucas."

He dropped my hand, put his hat on, and slid his coat on. "By the way, we hardly have to deal with snow in Ireland and won't have to wait until spring to keep working." He winked, then turned and headed down the hall, tipping his hat at Shawn who was walking up.

"Who is the old guy, and what was that about?"

I exhaled as I watched Dr. Martin walk away. I couldn't believe I was actually feeling torn. There was no way I would leave Hollie, but at the same time, I couldn't help but wonder if I was missing out on a once-in-a-lifetime opportunity.

Motioning for Shawn to come into my office, I softly shut the door and rounded my desk. I sat down and looked back out the window at the snow steadily coming down.

"Why do you look like someone just kicked your cat?" Shawn asked.

Turning to look at him, I gave a halfhearted laugh. "That was one of my Harvard professors. He works in the field now and is at a fairly new dig site in Ireland."

"Why was he here? Just in town and wanting to say hello?"

I shook my head. "No, he offered me a job."

That made Shawn sit up a bit. "What kind of a job?"

I felt my entire body sag; suddenly, I felt so damn tired. "The job of a lifetime."

"Damn," Shawn said. "Doing what?"

"Working in Ireland at a four-thousand-year-old burial site."

Shawn's eyes went wide with shock. "Holy shit, Lucas. What did you tell him?"

"No. I told him no."

"Why?" Shawn asked with a bewildered look. In the last week or so, he and Kristin had grown closer. According to Shawn, they were taking things slow and hadn't had sex, but they had done plenty of other things. Hollie thought it was funny they claimed to be moving slow when they were meeting for lunch nearly every day and doing things that might not have been intercourse but would still make a nun blush and ask for forgiveness.

"Did you really ask me that?"

He nodded. "I did. Lucas, for as long as I can remember, that's all you talked about. Digging in the damn dirt for old shit."

"And I do that now, here, at home. Near Hollie."

Shawn leaned back, a knowing look on his face as he slowly nodded. "I get it. You don't want to leave Hollie."

"Would you want to leave Kristin right as your relationship was growing? Or right when you were about to ask her to marry you?"

Shawn held up his hands. "Whoa, put the brakes on, dude."

"I'm talking about me, Shawn. Me! I'm going to be asking Hollie to marry me on Christmas day. I can't turn around and leave the country for months and expect her to drop her life here and go with me. And I sure as shit don't want to be away from her."

"It's called compromise, Lucas. You don't want Hollie to give up her life and career, but do think she'd want you to do that for her?"

"It's different. I have a job I love."

Shawn leaned forward and rested his forearms on his legs. "You're telling me that if you weren't with Hollie, you would still turn this job down?"

"I love my job!"

He tilted his head and stared at me.

Scrubbing my hand down my face, I let out a frustrated groan. "Fine! Fine! I'd probably ask for a leave of absence or something and go."

"So, the only thing holding you back is...Hollie."

"Don't say that. It makes it sound bad."

He held up his hand in defense. "I'm just shooting you straight here, dude. If you really wanted to do this, you'd think of a way, and if Hollie truly loves you, she'll let you pursue this job."

I glanced out the window once more and tried to ignore the sudden ache in the middle of my chest.

The sound of the front door shutting caused me to turn away from the back window I had been staring out of.

"Lucas?" Hollie called out.

"I'm in the back sunroom."

Hearing her heels click on the floor, I set my beer down and waited for my girl to come into the room. All I wanted to do was hold her.

"Oh, my gosh, have I had a day!" Hollie said as she stepped down into the room. Her face lit up the moment she saw me, and I couldn't ignore the way her smile still made my heart feel like it skipped a beat in my chest.

"I'm sorry," I said as I held out my arms. She instantly walked into them, then drew back and reached up to kiss me.

"It's okay. I'm just so glad that party is over and done with. Next year, I think I'm going to take the week before Christmas off." She tilted her head and kissed me once more. "I missed you."

Pushing a strand of brown hair behind her ear, I stared into those sky-blue eyes. "You just saw me this morning."

"And that was too long ago. I've only got Greg and Janet's party left, and then I'm in vacation mode. Well, there's the city Christmas party, but Mindy has that in hand. She's actually doing a wonderful job, and the suggestions she has made are wonderful. She's very talented."

"Everyone in the office was talking about how excited they are for the Christmas party."

Hollie's face beamed with happiness. "Really? That makes me so happy! When the mayor's wife found out I was doing the city Christmas party, she asked if I planned bridal showers. The mayor's wife, Lucas!"

Laughing, I drew her back against my body. "I'm so proud of you."

Her head dropped to my chest as she giggled. "It's just, I never imagined when I decided to start my own company that things would blow up like this. I'm going to enjoy it now before I have to step back from it all someday."

Frowning, I gently pushed her back some. "Why would you have to do that? Did you talk to Shawn?"

Laughing as she looked at me, confused, she asked, "Shawn? No, I was talking about someday when we decide to have kids."

Hollie kicked off her heels and then picked them up and set them to the side neatly. She was a neat freak at her house and mine.

"You think about us having kids?"

She looked at me and blushed. "I do, a lot, actually. A little baby Lucas and little Hollie might be fun."

"Might be? If they're anything like their mom, it will be an adventure."

Chuckling, she sat down on the sofa and pulled her feet up to her chest and wrapped her arms around them. "And just think, they could have Mommy's special powers."

I groaned and sat down next to her.

She sighed. "I was thinking of giving Mindy more events to plan."

"Really? You mean, have her plan them and not you?"

"Yep. I'd have to give the final approval on her plans, but she's talented, Lucas. I'd be stupid not to bring her on as more than my assistant."

"Wow, that's great."

We sat in silence for a minute or so. She bumped my arm, and I looked down at her. "What's going on?" she asked. "Bad day?"

I felt my brows draw in. "Not really, just a lot on my mind."

"You look tense. Is there anything I can do?"

Taking her hand, I kissed the back of it. "Nah, I'll figure it all out. I was thinking—do you want to go out to dinner tonight?"

Her eyes lit up. "Just us?"

"Just us," I said with a wink.

"Where?" she asked.

"I was thinking seafood. Maybe drive over to that new restaurant in Marblehead. It's right on the water and might be a nice sight to see with the snow."

Dropping her legs down, Hollie stood. "That's a great idea! Let me go get changed, and then we can leave."

Standing also, I followed her into the house as I headed to where my phone was charging. I had a text from Dr. Martin. When I opened it, it was a picture of the dig site. Unplugging it, I pushed it into my back pocket. The last thing I wanted to think about was his job offer.

After eating an amazing meal and sitting in the car watching the snow fall and cover the beach, I turned to Hollie and watched her for a moment. She was mesmerized by what she was seeing. I smiled and knew that she was the only woman I wanted to spend the rest of my life with. The only person I would lay my life down for. I also knew there was no way I would ever ask her to give up her dreams for me to follow my own. I loved her too much.

"A penny for your thoughts," I asked as I took her hand in mine and gave it a squeeze.

"It's so peaceful, and I was just thinking about how crazy the last month and a half has been. Then I started to think about how stressful it's going to be when we get back from vacation, with all the events I have."

"Did you not want to go on vacation?"

Her eyes widened. "Yes, I want to go on vacation. I need it more than I realized. I was thinking, though, I need a break. Some time off, and not just five days on a beach in the Caribbean, although that is going to be freaking amazing."

I chuckled. "It will be."

"I think I'm going to stop taking clients for a bit and let Mindy pick which events she'd like to plan."

My heart started to pound in my chest. "You're not thinking of walking away from your career, are you?"

She shook her head. "No, no. I'm going to let Mindy take on more projects, and I'll promote Joan to my assistant. Like I said earlier, I'll give Mindy the chance to plan the events with my final approval, and Joan can be more hands-on and work the events if the client asks. I want to be more of a consultant for a bit."

I closed my eyes and shook my head, attempting to figure out if I was awake or dreaming this. When I opened my eyes, she was looking back out over the beach. You could see the water simply from the reflection of the snow on the sand.

"Hollie, may I ask why, when you are literally making a name for yourself in Salem?"

She shrugged, not looking at me. "I don't think it will hurt me to step away from a bit, and something in here..." She put her hand over her heart. "...tells me I need to do this. I don't know why, but it's a strong feeling I have, and if I've learned anything these last few months, it's to listen to my intuition. And being here and watching the snow, I feel connected to it somehow. It's like..."

Her voice trailed off, and she smiled softly.

"It's like what?" I asked.

Turning to look at me, I saw something in those blue eyes I'd never seen before. A sort of peace that almost made me envious.

"It's like the snow is talking to me. I don't know how to describe it, and I'm sure you think I'm crazy."

Looking out over the beach, I couldn't help but sit in wonderment. Would I really be able to follow my dream and have Hollie by my side?

"Hollie?"

"Mmm?"

"Will you pinch me, so I know I'm awake?"

She giggled and then crawled over to sit on my lap. When she pushed down and rubbed over my instantly hard dick, she whispered, "I'll do ya one better."

"I like the sound of that."

Reaching between us, Hollie managed to unzip my pants and pulled me free while I pushed her panties to the side and played with her for a bit. She was already wet and ready.

"Take me, Hollie," I whispered as she bent her head, her brown hair falling around us, and I took my mouth with hers as she slowly slid down my cock. We both groaned as she rocked into me, rubbing her clit as her hand grabbed the back of my hair and jerked my head back. Her mouth moved down my neck as she moved faster.

"Hollie," I gasped as I held onto her ass, so fucking turned on. When she licked up my neck and bit my lower lip, I thought for sure I was going to come.

"Hollie, I can't... It feels too good."

"I'm almost there. Do it, Lucas. Do it!"

Confused, I drew back and looked at her. "Do what?"

"Your finger! Please!"

It only took me a moment to realize she wanted my finger up that tight ass of hers. All I had to do was barely slip it in, and Hollie exploded. The feel of her squeezing me caused me to come so damn hard, I was thanking the stars above we were parked in an empty parking lot, and it was pitch black out.

As Hollie came to a stop, she leaned her forehead to mine. Our breaths mingled with one another's as she let out the cutest-sounding giggle.

"I swear, I see lights flashing."

It was then, I noticed there really were lights flashing. Before either of us could do anything, a tap on my window had us both turning to see a cop standing there.

"Oh, shit," we both said as Hollie quickly attempted to climb off me. Her foot somehow got stuck in the steering wheel, and the horn started to go off.

"Hollie! You're on the horn!" I yelled.

"I'm stuck!"

I quickly tried to untangle her, only to have her knee me right in the balls.

"Oh, my God!" I cried out and dropped my head back on the seat. "Can't. Breathe."

"Okay, I'm out! I'm out!" Hollie cried out as she scrambled over to the other side of the car. I reached over and hit the window button as I tried to figure out how to breathe.

The cop leaned in, flashed his light right in my face, and grinned. "I saw that one coming."

Chapter Twelve

Hollie

"How does it feel to be a convicted criminal?"

I sighed for what felt like the millionth time as I attempted to ignore Kristin who was on the treadmill next to me. She was walking; I was running.

"Did you plead the fifth in jail too?"

Jumping to the sides of the treadmill, I glared at my best friend. "Will you stop calling me a criminal!"

She fought to hide her smile. "But you were in jail."

"For, like, ten minutes."

"Tell me again what your mom said! Please!"

As she lost it laughing, I started to run again. "I no longer consider you my best friend," I bit out. "Besides, I'm sure you already know everything. Shawn's dad is good friends with the cop who took us in."

Kristin wiped a pretend tear away. "Okay, you're right. Shawn did tell me everything. I don't understand—why did he arrest you guys?"

"You'd have to ask him," I panted out.

Kristin was silent, and I thanked God for that small miracle. It was short-lived.

"Couldn't you sense him? Or see it happening ahead of time?"

Stopping again, I hit the treadmill's off button, and it slowly came to a stop. "I was too busy having sex in the front seat of my boyfriend's car to notice if I had any...feelings other than the impending orgasm."

Kristin covered her mouth but burst out laughing again. When she finally was able to regain her composure, we walked over to the free weights.

I picked up some weights to work my arms.

"Shawn laughed nearly all night. Every time I fell asleep, he'd start laughing, and that would cause me to laugh."

"I'm so glad you two found it funny."

She picked up a weight and started working her triceps. "It was a bonding moment for us, I'm not going to lie."

Rolling my eyes, I put the weights down and used a bench to do dips.

She flopped down on the floor in front of me and took a long pull from her water bottle.

"Gross. Do you know how many people sweat, which drips to the floor?" I asked as I pushed up and sat on the bench. I wasn't in the mood to work out at all.

"One more question, and then I swear, I'll never bring it up again. I swear."

"Fine," I said. "One more and then I don't want to hear another word or laugh, giggle...nothing!"

Kristin lifted her hand, crossed her heart, and then gave some pledge with her fingers. I wasn't sure what that was about; she was never in the girl scouts.

"Was it worth it?"

I quickly glanced around as I felt my face heat.

"It was worth it," she answered for me. "I can see it written all over your face."

When I looked back at her, I tried to keep my giggle in but let out some weird sound with my lips before I covered my mouth. With a single nod, I dropped my hand. "So worth it."

She giggled like a little girl.

"Have you and Shawn crossed that line yet?"

"Nope."

"Really?" I asked, surprised. "I'm impressed. You guys are really taking this seriously."

"It doesn't hurt he likes his head between my legs and mine between his."

"Ugh. My gosh, Kristin! Really?" I glanced around and sighed in relief when I realized no one had heard her.

"What? I'm simply stating a fact. At this point, I say we go for it, but Shawn wants to make our second time more romantic than the first. I think it's sweet, but he better hurry his ass along. I'm losing my patience."

I laughed and stood. "I'm not in the mood to work out. Want to go last-minute Christmas shopping?"

"Hell, yes! I thought you would never ask!"

After showering and changing, we headed out into the frigid cold to do some shopping in downtown Salem. I had a few last-minute stocking stuffers I needed to get and had ordered a leather journal for Lucas I needed to pick up. Today was the last day before all the stores would be closed. It was for when he was out in the field working; he could write notes in it. Even with his dig site shut down for most of the winter, I knew he would love it when he would be able to use it. Right now, he used these little notebook pads, and they were everywhere.

"I'm surprised you're not at Rose's house making sure everything is ready for the bridal shower tonight."

I picked up the book that I had heard Tim, Lucas's father, mentioning he wanted to read, and decided to get it for him, along with a reading lamp he could clip onto the book. Rose mentioned more than once how Tim would keep her awake with the light on while he read before bed.

"This will be perfect," I mumbled to myself before I looked back at Kristin. "I stopped by yesterday and finished up most of the decorating. Mindy is there now making sure everything else is in place and ready to go."

Feeling her gaze on me, I looked up at her. "What?"

She gave a one-shoulder shrug. "Nothing. I'm just surprised you're letting your assistant handle that."

"She can handle it, and I promoted her. She's no longer my assistant but an associate planner. Most of the setup was yesterday, and I was there for that. Today is more like a test for her. If I decide to take a few months off, then I'll know whether she and Joan will be able to handle it."

"So, Lucas talked to you about Ireland then?"

I paused before I picked up a vase, I thought my mother would love. Turning my head, I gave Kristin a questioning look. "Ireland?"

By the look on her face, it was clear she had made a blunder. I was instantly curious. The photos that Lucas had been studying were from Ireland. "What are you talking about?"

Spinning away from me, she was suddenly very interested in a crocheted wine holder. "Oh, look at this. How...um... how different."

"Kristin," I said in a calm but stern voice, "what do you mean, he talked to me about Ireland?"

Dropping the wine holder back on the table, she spun back around, a horrified look on her face. "Shawn told me, but I don't think he was supposed to tell anyone, and he made me promise I wouldn't say anything to you, but when you started talking about taking time off, I just naturally assumed Lucas had told you and that you had agreed it was a good idea and that was why…" She sucked in a deep breath and went on. "…you said you were taking some time off. I thought it was to go to Ireland."

"Why would I go to Ireland?" I patiently asked, even though inside, I was pretty sure I knew why.

Chewing on her lower lip, she shook her head. "Can you not just forget the last, like, three minutes? I'll totally buy you whatever you want. Anything! Even this, um, cute little wine holder thingy."

My arms crossed over my chest. Well, they tried to. I had my coat draped over one arm. "Spill it, Kristin."

She shook her head. "No, please don't ask me to, Hollie. It needs to come from Lucas and not second-hand."

"Is Lucas going to Ireland?"

She shrugged.

"Why is he going to Ireland?"

Another shrug.

"Is it for his work?"

Her mouth twitched, and this time, it was half of a one-shoulder shrug.

"Oh, my God. Did he get another job?"

That time, she only made a scrunched-up face.

"He was offered another job, but he isn't sure he wants to take it…because it's in Ireland!"

Kristin tilted her head. "I wonder, do you think that's why we're such good friends? You know, the whole 'you're a witch and I'm a witch' connection we have going on?"

Ignoring her, I went on. "That explains why he's been so off. And the feeling I had to take some time away."

"You had a feeling?" she asked in a curious tone.

I nodded. "Yeah, the night at the beach as I was watching the snow fall, a strange sensation came over me that I needed to take some time off. I mean, I am exhausted. The last few months have been crazy-busy, and I'm not complaining. But the feeling was so strong. Now I know why. Lucas was offered something away from me. He's torn because he doesn't want to leave, and I know Lucas. He would never ask me to walk away from my own goals and dreams."

"And you're okay doing that? I mean, if he decides to go, you'd go and leave your company behind."

Thinking about her words, I drew in a slow, deep breath and exhaled. "I wouldn't look at it as leaving my company behind. I've worked for years to grow it, and I'm happy to see it expanding. At the same time, since meeting Lucas, I've come to realize there are other things in my life that I want to focus on."

"Like?" she asked, both brows raised.

"Like getting married someday. Have a baby or maybe two. Work on my craft. I have these amazing gifts I've kept buried down for so many years, and I want to learn more about them. Since getting in touch with my inner self, I've become so aware of my surroundings. Of what the world is telling me. I don't want to be a slave to my job, I want to enjoy my life. I can still work and have that. And the only way for me to do that is to learn to step back and let other people help me achieve my goals. And if this trip to Ireland is something Lucas truly wants, then I want to support him."

Frowning, I pursed my lips, then said, "But he actually has to tell me about it."

Kristin took my hand in hers. "He will. Maybe he's trying to let it all soak in himself. But Shawn did say Lucas told them no."

"Really?"

She nodded. "I think they gave him until, like, the twenty-seventh to decide."

I exhaled. It was Christmas Eve. That meant time was running out for Lucas to tell me.

Deciding to talk to him tomorrow since tonight was the bridal shower, I looked back down at the table. "I think I'm going to get this vase and then call it a day. After all, we have a bridal shower to get ready for tonight."

"Oh, I meant to ask you: Is Wendy going to be there? I haven't seen her around."

Looking at Kristin, I shook my head. "I can't believe I didn't tell you!"

Kristin's eyes lit up with glee. She had always been one for a good bit of gossip. "Tell me what?"

"She moved!"

"Whaaat?"

I laughed. "I know! She moved to New York City. Said she wanted to explore new opportunities. She RSVP'd she wouldn't be at the shower."

"Wow. I didn't see that coming. Oh, well, at least you won't have to deal with that awkwardness."

"Tell me about it."

"Did Lucas ever tell his parents about what happened?"

With a shake of my head, I replied, "Nope. But he did tell Greg, who told Janet. Needless to say, she wasn't upset her sister was going to be MIA during the shower."

Kristin chuckled. "I always did like that Janet."

"Me too!" I agreed as we locked arms and giggled the entire way to the cashier.

Chapter Thirteen

Hollie

Rose caught me right as I was popping a hors d'oeuvre into my mouth. She pulled me into her arms and hugged me so tightly, I nearly popped the food out of my mouth.

"Everything looks beautiful, sweetheart! Just beautiful. You truly have such a talent for party planning."

Smiling, I forced the piece of cheese and meat down.

"Thank you, Rose. I'm so glad you're happy with it." Glancing around the room, I spied Janet. "Janet seems to be happy as well. She looks beautiful."

"Yes, she does. As do you. There is a glow about you this evening."

Placing my hand on the side of my face, I chuckled. "Probably the wine."

"Everyone is gushing about the tables. I love how you used the square white vases and put the flowers and greenery in them. And the floating candles are stunning. I'm not sure how you did it, but they are beautiful."

"It's easy. You just use gel beads, put the decorations

111

you want in the vase, then pour water in. They give the appearance of floating in the vase."

"Stunning," Rose said as she looked around the room.

"You're happy with the caterer?"

Rose put her hand to her heart. "Yes! Did you see that tree charcuterie board?"

Laughing, I nodded. "I did."

"They told me you asked for that design."

Another nod. "I did. I saw a picture on Pinterest and I loved it. Showed it to them and asked if they could do it."

"Greg's favorite thing is how you used little toy soldiers as the nameplates. How did you know he loved them?"

"Lucas," I answered with a wide grin.

"Of course! Of course!" She squeezed my arm. "I better get back to the guests."

"I'm going to stick by this table here and eat some more!"

Rose laughed as she drifted away.

I reached for another toothpick of yummies when my entire body heated. Without even turning around, I said, "I was wondering when you would break away from Janet's parents."

A low chuckle came, followed by warm breath on my neck.

"You look so freaking hot in this red dress."

Tilting my head to give him better access, Lucas placed a kiss on my neck.

"Mmm, I believe you've told me once or twice."

"It's the truth, and it's driving me crazy. When can we leave?"

Turning, I pushed an olive into his mouth. "Not until it's over, or at least until after we finish dinner."

He dropped his shoulders and groaned.

I patted his chest. "It's not so bad."

Lucas smiled. "The house and the room are beautiful, Hollie. I'm so very proud of you, I hope you know that. And I would never ask you to..."

His voice trailed off.

"Ask me to what?"

With a tight smile, he lifted my hand and kissed the back of it. He had a habit of doing that, and I loved it. Sometimes he switched it up and kissed my wrist, which turned me on like crazy.

"I'm just so damn proud of you. I don't tell you nearly enough."

My heart melted, and my knees went weak. I hated to see the conflict in his eyes; the only thing I wanted to do was take it away. The best way to do that was to be honest.

"I know about Ireland."

The color from his face drained. "Is that why you said you wanted to take a break? I would never in a million years ask you to step away from your career or your life here in Salem, or—"

"Let me rephrase that. I know you've been stressing about something to do with Ireland, but I'm not sure exactly what it is. And to answer your question, no. I had no idea until today."

He narrowed one eye suspiciously. "Shawn told you?"

"No, Kristin. Apparently, their relationship has moved to sharing secrets."

Lucas rolled his eyes. "I was planning on talking to you about it tonight, I swear. I just wasn't sure it was something I even wanted to do."

Taking his hands in mine, I smiled up at him. "We can talk about it after the shower, but know one thing, Lucas Dayton. I love you with my heart and soul, and I know you would never ask me to do something unless it meant a lot to you. I'm home when I'm with you. You are my safe place. The only place I want to be. Everything else is a bonus."

He dropped my hands and cupped my face. "How did I get so lucky to have you love me? And why did we waste all those years being so stupid?"

I giggled. "Hardheaded, I guess."

He ran his thumb over my lower lip. "I love you so much, Hollie. More than you'll ever know."

Reaching up, I kissed him softly. "I think I know because I feel the same."

He studied my face, then dropped his eyes to my mouth, then moved them back up again. He shook his head. "I can't wait. I can't wait to do it."

"What?" I asked, confused as he took my hand and then pulled me through his parents' house, past onlookers who were just as shocked as I was as Lucas practically ran through the house with me trailing behind him.

"Excuse me. Excuse us," I said as I gave a smile of apology to the number of people who he nearly knocked over.

Walking into the mud room, Lucas reached for my coat and then slipped it on me. He put his coat on and held the back door open, motioning for me to go outside. Once outside, we headed toward his parents' gazebo.

"Lucas, slow down! Do you know how hard it is to walk in heels even with the sidewalk cleared of snow!"

Stopping, he turned and swept me up into his arms as I let out a shriek of laughter.

He stepped up into the gazebo, then slowly set me down. It was chilly, but Rose had drapes that hung down, and Lucas pulled the two closed, then reached for the small heater. Rose had arranged for the gazebo to be heated in case anyone wanted to slip away. I was pretty sure she hadn't planned on her son losing his mind, though.

Lucas drew my coat closed, then kissed me as if he hadn't seen me in a month.

When he drew back and looked into my eyes, I swayed. "Wow. What was that for?"

Then he reached into his pocket and pulled out a small box, got down on his knee, and opened it. Tears clouded my eyes, and I took a few steps back, my hand over my mouth as a sob forced its way out. Then I broke down crying before I launched myself into his body, damn near knocking him over. I didn't even care that I heard my dress rip.

With my arms wrapped tightly around him, I cried into his neck.

He held me close and said, "Don't cry, angel. Please don't cry."

Pulling back to look at him, I spoke between sobs. "Yes, oh, my gosh, yes!"

He laughed. "I haven't even asked yet."

"I don't care!" I cried out. "The answer is yes!"

Wrapping my arms around him again, I cried tears of happiness. When I finally got myself settled down, Lucas helped me stand, and we sat on the bench in the gazebo.

"This ring," he said as he took it out of the box and slipped it onto my finger, "was my great-grandmother's. My father gave it to me. My mom wanted a yellow diamond, so he saved this for whichever of his kids would want it. I lucked out."

I wiped the tears from my face as I got a better look at the stunningly beautiful round diamond with the double halo of smaller diamonds. There was a crisscross pattern down the side, and it was set in what I thought was white gold. I couldn't stop staring at it.

"Is it white gold?"

"Platinum."

My eyes shot up to his. "Lucas, this ring must be worth a small fortune. Are you sure...?"

"Look at it again, Hollie. It fits you like it was made for you."

Tearing up again, I held it up and gasped once more. "I've never seen anything so beautiful in my entire life."

He smiled.

"I had this whole beautiful night planned on Christmas, and I was going to ask you then. Even bought a Christmas bulb to put the ring in. Shawn and Kristin are going to be pissed because they had planned on setting up the house for when I asked."

I laughed and another sob slipped free. "No, I love that you did it in the moment. It means so much more to me."

"Are you cold? Should we go back in?"

Shaking my head, I replied, "No. The little heater is working great. What made you decide to ask me tonight? Out of the blue like that."

He looked down, and I could tell he was nervous. With a deep breath in, he looked at me. "An old college professor of mine stopped by my office the other day. He asked if I wanted to help head up a dig site in Ireland. It's a four-thousand-year-old Bronze Age burial site. It's a rare find and an archaeologist's dream come true. I love my job here in Salem, but this...this is why I became an archaeologist. He wants me to leave two days after Christmas, and it would be at least a six-to-eight-month commitment. At first, my reply was no."

"Why would you say no if this is something you've always dreamed of?"

"I didn't want to leave you, and I would never ask you to just up and leave your life here for months on end. Not when you've been doing so good."

Taking his hand in mine, I said, "Lucas, our relationship is going to be about give and take. If I'm giving now,

I'm positive there will be a time when I'm taking and you're giving. It's about compromise and doing what makes each other happy. Right now, I simply want to be with you. I know you'll be busy probably each day, but we'll be together and in Ireland!"

A wide smile broke across his face. "You can even help at the site if you want."

I perked up. "Would I get to have my own little brush to use?"

Lucas laughed. "I'll get you your very own kit. How's that?"

"With my name on it?"

He nodded as he wore a wide smile.

"It's like what I said earlier, my home is where you are, Lucas."

He kissed my wrist, and my stomach fluttered. "My home is where you are as well."

"So, are we going to do this?"

"Wait—what about the parties you already have planned? We won't be here for New Year's."

Stopping for a moment to think, the answer popped into my head. "Why don't you go first since we'll need a place to live? I'll finish out this year's parties and then let my customers know I'll be leaving, but I'll still be available to help plan. It just won't be hands-on. Then I can come and join you in Ireland."

He slowly shook his head as if he were in awe. "Are you sure, Hollie?"

My hand slipped behind his neck, and I drew him to me. With our mouths inches apart, I whispered, "I'm sure."

The look on his face was one of utter joy. He almost looked like a little boy set free in a toy store.

"What about your job?" I asked.

"I spoke with the city manager and asked if I could take a leave of absence for the project. He basically told me not to give up this opportunity and felt it would strengthen my knowledge. My job will be here for me when I get back."

I smiled. "Then it's settled. We're going to Ireland."

Lucas stood and pulled me up with him. He drew me to him and kissed me so passionately, I nearly begged him to take me right there in the gazebo. I know for a fact, Rose hadn't planned on that!

"We should get back in. I'm sure you're freezing," he said, his forehead against mine.

"I say, we sneak away and tell everyone I wasn't feeling well."

A wicked, sexy smile appeared, and before I knew it, I was being carried through the backyard, down the side of the house, and being placed in the passenger seat of Lucas's car.

"Thank God no one blocked us in!" he said as he got in and headed toward his house.

The entire car ride, all I could do was stare at my beautiful ring. I had never in my life been as happy as I was in that moment.

Chapter Fourteen

Lucas

Drawing in a deep breath, I took in the cool, damp air while I drank my coffee and looked over the site where we were digging. The area that the site had been found in was part of a tunnel system connecting Dublin with Galway on the other side of the island. It had been a controversial project to start with, and now, with this find, there were talks of scrapping it altogether. The island wasn't that big, and to be honest, it was so beautiful here, I couldn't imagine who wouldn't enjoy the drive.

"I cannot believe we found so much burned flint," Matt Leiver said. He was one of the consultant archaeologists who worked for Dublin Archaeology.

With a nod, I replied, "I'm thinking leathermaking."

He rubbed his chin. "And metal work. God, wouldn't you love to go back in time and see how they lived?"

I smiled. "I would indeed."

I'd been in Ireland for nearly a month, and Hollie was due to arrive next week. I couldn't wait to see her. We talked every morning and night, no matter what time it was for either of us. Seeing her over FaceTime wasn't nearly good enough. I wanted to hold her, show her how much I loved and missed her. We'd gotten creative a few times with Face-Time sex, something I would highly recommend to everyone.

"Lucas! Matt!" a voice called from our right. "You've got to see this!"

Setting my coffee down, I followed Matt as we rushed to one of the areas where we had been working. I was almost positive the area had been a structure at one time.

Coming to a stop, my mouth dropped open at the site before me.

"Holy shit, you were right," Matt whispered. "It's the base of some kind of structure."

I quickly jumped into work mode. We needed to proceed carefully; hopefully, we'd find an artifact that would tell us what the site was used for.

"Look—this looks like a pot, maybe?" Ryan, another archeologist from London, said.

I nearly jumped with excitement as the whole team started to carefully clear the area around the pot. After a few hours, the pot has been carefully removed and placed in a container to bring back to the onsite lab, where it would be examined and then carefully cleaned.

When I felt my phone buzz in my back pocket, I stood and stretched. Christ, I'd been bent over for so long, I was stiff as a board.

Taking the phone out, I smiled when I saw who had texted me.

Hollie: How is your day going?

I quickly typed back my reply.

Me: Amazing! We found an area that looks to have been a structure of some sort. We got one pot out,

and there is another piece that looks like part of a sword maybe.

Hollie: Ohhh, that sounds interesting. So, not just a gravesite?

Laughing, I shook my head.

Me: Nope. I'm hoping we can make at least one more discovery before we lose daylight.

Hollie: I have a feeling you're going to make a pretty big one, maybe even two.

My heart jumped. Had she had a vision?

Me: What makes you say that?

When my phone rang, I jumped.

"Hey, is everything okay?" I asked. Hollie never called when I was at the site.

"Turn around and make your first discovery."

Confused, I turned and saw her standing by one of the tents. Her long, brown hair was in a ponytail, but it whipped in the wind as she lifted her hand and waved.

"You're here! You're not supposed to be for another week."

She chuckled. "I didn't want to wait another week."

"I'll be right there."

Hitting End, I turned to Matt and Ryan. "I'm taking a break. My fiancé is here a week early."

Ryan grinned. "Dude, take the rest of the day off. We don't have much sun left anyway."

Nodding, I said, "I might just do that."

"Perks of being the boss," Matt said with a wink.

I quickly walked toward Hollie, fighting the urge to sprint. The last thing I wanted was for everyone to see me running toward her, even though that was all I wanted to do.

Stopping in front of her, I watched her blue eyes catch my brown.

"You're here."

She smiled. "I'm here."

I drew her to me and hugged her, picking her up and spinning her around. The sound of her laughter filled my heart with so much joy.

"Is everything okay at home?"

She nodded. "Well, at your mom's birthday party the other day, your Aunt Nancy showed everyone her flamingo dance. She truly is convinced she was one in a prior life. She even asked me if I read tarot cards and could tell her if I saw her in another life."

I rolled my eyes.

"Come on, I'm taking the rest of the day off. You're probably exhausted."

She smiled slightly and said, "Yeah, I could try and eat something. I haven't been feeling all myself lately."

With her hand in mine, we walked through the tent. "What's wrong? Stressed about the move?"

"No," she chuckled. "It's not that."

We had to stop a few times in order for me to introduce Hollie to some people, and when we finally got to the rental car I'd been driving, I could tell Hollie was about to pass out.

"Did you not sleep on the flight at all?"

"I slept some."

Hollie walked to the wrong side of the car and laughed when she opened it. I held open her door. "Wait, where is your luggage?"

"It's already at the flat. I stopped there first."

"Perfect. I've got some stuff to make something to eat, or we could go out."

"Let's stay in," she said.

"That sounds like a plan."

As we drove down the winding road, I kept noticing Hollie put her hand up to her neck or her stomach. Shit, I really hoped she wasn't coming down with something.

The moment I pulled into the driveway, she jumped out of the car and rushed to the front door. I had to jog to catch up to her. I unlocked the front door, and Hollie pushed past me and ran to the bathroom, and I followed.

"Hollie, are you okay...? Oh, gross!" I said as Hollie leaned over and puked. And puked. And puked some more.

Then she stood there, leaning over the toilet with dry heaves.

I had run and gotten a washcloth and handed it to her. She placed it over her entire face as I rubbed her back.

"Did you eat something bad on the plane, you think?"

Hollie slowly stood. She rinsed out her mouth, then took my hand as I led her straight to the bedroom, where she promptly crawled onto the bed.

"No, it's not that."

"The flu?"

She shook her head.

I felt her forehead; no fever.

"How long have you been sick?"

"Oh, awhile."

"Have you gone to the doctor?"

With a nod, she said, "Yep."

"What did they say?"

"Can you grab my purse? I dropped it on the way in."

Kissing her on the forehead, I replied, "Of course. Let me go get it."

I came back with her purse and set it next to her. She dug around and pulled out a little yellow envelope that had my name on it and handed it to me.

"What's this?"

Sitting up, Hollie pulled her legs up and rested her chin on her knees. The color slowly started to come to her beautiful face. She grinned and said, "Open it."

I shot a curious look in her direction, to which she responded by motioning at the envelope. "Just open it, will you?"

I slid my finger under the flap, pulled out the card, and opened it. I stared at what was inside of it for what felt like forever, then I turned back to her and watched as a tear traveled down her cheek.

"Hollie."

Her hand came up to her mouth to hold back her sob.

I dropped the card and piece of paper that was inside and pulled her to me and went to kiss her.

"I have to brush my teeth! I threw up, Lucas!"

Ignoring the way she kept trying to avoid my mouth, I cupped her face and stared into her eyes.

"A baby."

She nodded and more tears slipped free. "A baby."

Find out what happens next on March 17, 2023, in

Other Books by Kelly Elliott

Other Books by Kelly Elliott
Holidaze in Salem
A Bit of Hocus Pocus
A Bit of Holly Jolly
A Bit of Wee Luck – March 2023
A Bit of Razzle Dazzle – July 4, 2023

Love in Montana
Fearless Enough – March 21, 2023
Cherished Enough – June 6, 2023
Brave Enough – August 29, 2023
Daring Enough – November 21, 2023
Loved Enough – February 6, 2024
Forever Enough – April 30, 2024
Enchanted Enough – July 23, 2024
Perfect Enough – October 15, 2024
Devoted Enough – January 7, 2025

The Seaside Chronicles
Returning Home*
Part of Me*
Lost to You
Someone to Love - January 3, 2023
*Available on audiobook at time of print

Stand Alones

The Journey Home*
Who We Were*
The Playbook*
Made for You*
*Available on audiobook

Boggy Creek Valley Series

The Butterfly Effect*
Playing with Words*
She's the One*
Surrender to Me*
Hearts in Motion*
Looking for You*
Surprise Novella TBD
*Available on audiobook

Meet Me in Montana Series

Never Enough*
Always Enough*
Good Enough*
Strong Enough*
*Available on audiobook

Southern Bride Series

Love at First Sight*
Delicate Promises*
Divided Interests*
Lucky in Love*
Feels Like Home *
Take Me Away*
Fool for You*
Fated Hearts*
*Available on audiobook

Cowboys and Angels Series

*Lost Love**
*Love Profound**
*Tempting Love**
*Love Again**
*Blind Love**
*This Love**
*Reckless Love**
*Available on audiobook

Boston Love Series

Searching for Harmony
Fighting for Love
*Series available on audiobook

Austin Singles Series

Seduce Me
Entice Me
Adore Me
*Series available on audiobook

Wanted Series

*Wanted**
*Saved**
*Faithful**
Believe
*Cherished**
*A Forever Love**
The Wanted Short Stories
All They Wanted
*Available on audiobook

Love Wanted in Texas Series

Spin-off series to the WANTED Series

Without You

Saving You

Holding You

Finding You

Chasing You

Loving You

Entire series available on audiobook

*Please note *Loving You* combines the last book of the Broken and Love Wanted in Texas series.

Broken Series

Broken*

Broken Dreams*

Broken Promises*

Broken Love

*Available on audiobook

The Journey of Love Series

Unconditional Love

Undeniable Love

Unforgettable Love

*Entire series available on audiobook

With Me Series

Stay With Me

Only With Me

*Series available on audiobook

Speed Series

Ignite

Adrenaline

*Series available on audiobook or coming to audiobook soon

COLLABORATIONS

Predestined Hearts (co-written with Kristin Mayer)*

*Play Me (*co-written with Kristin Mayer)*

*Dangerous Temptations (*co-written with Kristin Mayer*

*Available on audiobook